Rook 4:

SNOWMAN

Rook 4:
SNOWMAN

Graham Masterton

This first world edition published in Great Britain 1999 by
SEVERN HOUSE PUBLISHERS LTD of
9–15 High Street, Sutton, Surrey SM1 1DF.
This title first published in the U.S.A. 2000 by
SEVERN HOUSE PUBLISHERS INC of
595 Madison Avenue, New York, N.Y. 10022.

British Library Cataloguing in Publication Data

Masterton, Graham, 1946-
    Rook
    4: Snowman
    1. Horror tales
    I. Title
    823.9'14 [F]

    ISBN 0-7278-5427-5

Typeset in Great Britain by Palimpsest Book Production Ltd
Polmont, Stirlingshire, Scotland.
Printed and bound in Great Britain by
MPG Books Ltd, Bodmin, Cornwall.

One

With a chorus of high-pitched screams from his balding tires, Jim Rook drove into the parking lot at West Grove Community College in his old bronze Cadillac convertible and bounced to a stop in the Dean's personal parking space. He climbed out of the car without opening the door, caught his shoe on the handle, and dropped his file of homework, scattering papers all over the tarmac and into the bushes.

He was fifteen minutes late for his first class already, and he hopped around the parking lot stamping on sheets of paper to stop them from blowing away. It was a glaring hot day in early June, but there was a nagging southerly breeze, and it took an inspired jump over a jacaranda bush to stop Linda Starewsky's essay on *Hamlet* from being blown away across the college grounds and into the trees. Not that it would have been any great loss to critical literature.

"Hey, Mr Rook! Didn't know you white folks were so good at dancing!" called out Clarence, the janitor, as he passed by with his little sweeping-pan and the scraper he used for removing warm Bubblicious from the sidewalks.

Jim was in too much of a hurry to think of a smart reply. He shouldered his way through the side doors of the college, cramming his papers in a big untidy bunch under his arm. He jogged as far as the main corridor, his untied laces whipping the floor. Then he slowed down to a hurried hobble. He was

1

too breathless and dehydrated to force himself any further. He had woken up nearly an hour late with a hangover the size of Mount Rushmore, and he had left his apartment without even a swig of flat Gatorade. He had been trapped on the freeway in a sea of glittering metal for over a half-hour, breathing in eight lanes of yellow traffic fumes, with the morning sun beating on his forehead.

He reached a water-fountain and bent over it. He was still wearing his sunglasses and he hit his head against the wall. He opened his mouth; but instead of water he found himself sucking something slippery and hard and intensely cold. He said, "What the – *phhwah!*" and jerked his head up, spitting in disgust. He took off his Ray-Bans. The water was curving out of the spout in a crystal-clear arc. *Still* curving, even though he wasn't pressing the lever any more. He looked closer and realized that it wasn't moving. He tentatively reached out with his finger and prodded it, and it was ice.

He looked around, bewildered. The corridor was deserted. The college was air-conditioned, and comparatively cool, but how could the water in the fountain have frozen solid? He snapped it off and turned it this way and that, between his fingers.

He was still examining it when the swing doors at the far end of the corridor banged open and the new head of English came lolloping toward him. Dr Bruce Friendly was a big-boned, surly, loosely built man, with a high shock of wiry white hair. He walked everywhere like a giant-sized marionette, throwing one foot in front of the other as if he were trying to shake it off.

He had intense, near-together eyes and intense, near-together ideas. One of those ideas was that teaching high-flown English literature to a bunch of dyslexics and Hispanics and characters out of a Spike Lee movie was a waste of Los Angeles public taxes that bordered on the criminal. If

2

Jim's English and Special Needs Class hadn't impressed the Japanese education minister so much on his recent trip to California, Dr Friendly would have axed it as his second most urgent priority after ordering himself a high-backed tilt-swivel chair with a view of the girls' tennis courts.

'He's Japanese! What does he know about English? The guy speaks in squiggles.'

Jim was still staring into the open palm of his hand when Dean Friendly came up and stood right beside him him and stared into his hand, too.

"What do you make of that?" asked Jim.

"I don't follow you, James. What do I make of the fact that the palm of your hand is wet? I'd guess you were sweating because you're running way behind time and your class sounds like the second battle of Antietam."

"Well, it's wet now, but it a few seconds ago it was *ice.*"

Dr Friendly stared at him without any pretense of interest or sympathy. "I've told you what I think about what you do. If the education board didn't think that you were such a glittering public-relations asset, I'd have your contract terminated tomorrow and your class out doing what they were born to do, which is fix automobiles, serve in hamburger restaurants and sweep up trash. Sometimes you ought to stop and think what a great service you're giving to the community, James! Teaching Shakespeare to a motley collection of kids who can't even spell their own names!"

"What's wrong with that? Shakespeare couldn't spell his own name, either."

"The day that one of your students writes anything half as good as *Troilus and Cressida*, I'll let him spell his goddamned name any way he likes."

Jim continued to hold open the palm of his hand. "I don't

actually want to get into a discussion about Special Class II. This was ice. The water-fountain was frozen."

"Well, maybe we're having a little trouble with the water-refrigeration unit. Why don't you mention it to maintenance?"

"Even if the water-refrigeration unit was on the fritz, how could the water freeze in mid-air? It was there, in a curve, just *frozen*."

"Did you go to a *party* last night?" asked Dr Friendly, peering at him closely. "You look as if you went to a party last night. How can I guess that? The bags under the eyes? The stubble, perhaps? The hog's breath?"

"I went to a party last night, yes sir. In fact I *held* a party last night. It was my housewarming. I just moved into a new apartment. One block from the boardwalk, with a glorious view of the ocean, so long as you stand on the bathroom window-ledge with a mirror attached to a walking-stick, and bend your head backward, like *this*."

Dr Friendly watched him bend his head backward like *this*, and remained totally unimpressed. "How much did you drink during this housewarming?"

"Not much. Why? I might have toyed with one or two tequila slammers."

"Yes?"

"I might even have drunk two or three beers, or was it four? And somebody brought a case of sparkling wine. It was a celebration, what do you expect? New apartment, new me. I'm thinking of buying a dog, too. A schnauzer. I might call it Dr Friendly, after you."

Dr Friendly took hold of Jim's hand and held it up. "Did you really see ice, James? Or are you still under the influence? I'd be only too pleased to report you for showing up at college unfit for teaching duties."

"Excuse me, sir. I'm as fit for my teaching duties as you

are." He looked down at Dr Friendly's protruding stomach. "And trimmer, I hope."

"Then tuck in your shirt-tail and get along to that collection of dummies you call a class."

Jim looked away for a moment, with his hand pressed to his mouth. Then he turned back and said, "Listen, sir. You've made it one hundred per cent clear that you don't like me and you don't see the point of my class. You're the head of the English department and you're entitled to your own personal opinions, even if they are bigoted and intolerant and narrow-minded and educationally unsound. But my class is made up of young people who have had enough of a struggle in their lives already, without being dragged down and demeaned by the very people who are supposed to be helping them. They have speech impediments to overcome; they have cognitive difficulties; and almost all of them come from crummy rundown homes where they're the only ones who know how to read and write, and if they so much as pick up a book even their own parents make them feel like they're freaks. So if you want to insult me personally, go ahead. Call me anything you want. But never, ever call my students 'dummies', never again."

Dr Friendly took a deep, slow breath and his mouth puckered up. "I think you'd better get yourself off to that oh-so-needy class of yours, don't you, before you say something you wish you hadn't? And by the way, your new student has started today. Hubbard, from Alaska. Half Inuit, half idiot, from what I can make out. I wish you joy of him."

Jim didn't trust himself to say anything else. He knew that his remedial English class wasn't universally popular. Several members of the faculty believed that he was giving his pupils a hope of social betterment which they would never be able to achieve, and which would lead them to become even more disenchanted with the world than they were already. There were times when he had toe-to-toe arguments with other members of the faculty and enjoyed it: they fired up his adrenalin. But Dr Friendly was so unremittingly hostile that he could have happily taken hold of his stringy bolo necktie and twisted it around until his big horse-like face turned purple.

He turned the next corner and even though his classroom door was closed he could hear that Dr Friendly was right about the noise. Some of the class were whooping and laughing while others were attempting their own nasal versions of this week's chart hits and three black girls were singing 'I Will Always Love You' in a harmonized scream. Jim came in through the door and walked over to his desk, dropping his homework on it in a heap. As he did so, the class instantly fell quiet.

He stood and looked at them for a while, saying nothing, as if he had just arrived by time machine and was wondering which century this was and who all these weirdly dressed young people were, with their extraordinary hair and rings in their noses.

They looked back at him with equal uncertainty: a disheveled thirty-six-year-old in dark aviator sunglasses and a crumpled brown shirt with turquoise surfers on it. His steel-banded wristwatch was too big for his skinny wrist. His khaki docker pants looked as if he had used them as a pillow. Despite an attempt to paste it down with water, his hair stuck up at the back like a cockatoo. He hadn't shaved.

Slowly, he took off his sunglasses.

"*Boy*," said Washington Freeman III, a hugely tall black boy who always sat in the front row. "You look like you met Godzilla on your way to class."

"That's not a very respectful way to talk about Dr Friendly," said Jim, without even the flicker of a smile.

"Heck, I didn't mean that," grinned Washington. "I meant you look like *shit*."

"What does that mean, I look like shit?" Jim demanded. He stepped up to Washington and craned his neck back so that he could look him directly in the eye. "You mean I'm chocolatey-brown and steaming, what?"

"Well, no, sir, all I meant was—"

"Shit is a lazy and woolly way of expressing yourself, apart from being offensive. What are you going to write in your next essay? 'Hamlet's father came to the feast and he looked like shit'? How many marks do you think they'd award you for that?"

"But it don't mean shit like *shit* shit. It mean just, you know, like *shit*, and shit."

"You're not thinking of compiling a dictionary when you leave college, are you? Listen, Washington, anybody who has a half-reasonable grasp of thc English language never has to use words like shit. You could say I was pallid, haggard, worn, ravaged or unlovely. You could say that I was white as a ghost, wrinkled as prune or crumpled as a sheet of wrapping paper. You could describe my face as looking like an unmade bed or two pounds of condemned veal or a wedding-cake that has been left out in the rain. All of which are well-known literary descriptions."

He walked slowly between the lines of desks, looking one by one at his eighteen students. White, black, Hispanic, Chinese: all of them disadvantaged not only by poverty and social class, but by basic reading problems and stutters and word-blindness and a lack of concentration that would have embarrassed a gnat.

"Better still," he said, "you could invent your own description of the way I look. You could coin a new

7

phrase, so that you conjure up in other people's minds a vivid picture that describes me even more clearly than a photograph. In fact, since I not only look like shit but I feel like shit, that's going to be your first project for this morning. Describe my hungover appearance in not more than twelve well-chosen words."

There was a general groan of complaint and somebody threw a paper pellet at Washington and hit him on top of the head. "Keep your mo' close nex' time, short-ass."

Jim returned to his desk, tucking in his shirt. Suzie Wintz winked at him and said, "Hi, Mr Rook. Looks like you partied pretty hard last night." Suzie always looked fashion-magazine perfect. She had heaps of curly blonde hair and huge mint-green eyes and a permanent pout. She always described herself as 'trainee mode'. But for all of her confidence and all of her sensuality, she could barely write more than three consecutive sentences, one of the most memorable of which had been 'Shakespeare was balled and rote plas like Titanic'.

"There are three occasions in his life when a man is duty-bound to party," Jim told her, sorting through his homework. "The first is when his voice breaks. The second is when he's just about to get married. The third is when he realizes that life is one-third getting yourself together and two-thirds slowly falling apart again."

"You just made that up."

"Yes. Clever of me, wasn't it? Now *you* make up a good descriptive phrase for the way I look, just like I asked you to."

He turned his attention at last to the boy slouching in his chair two desks behind Linda Starewsky. At first sight, he looked unusually mature and handsome compared with most of Jim's students. At this age, most of them still had small heads and big noses and protruding ears and constellations of bright red spots. Jim called them 'Quarks' after the alien character in *Star Trek*. But this boy had a chiseled, adult-looking face, with high cheekbones and a straight nose and a very firm jawline. His black hair was cut *en brosse* and he had startlingly blue eyes. He wore a very white T-shirt with *Anchorage, Alaska* emblazoned on the front, washed-out blue jeans and very expensive Timberland boots. He had an olive-skinned sulkiness about him which put Jim in mind of a young Elvis Presley.

"So, you're Jack Hubbard," said Jim, approaching him and holding out his hand. "Welcome to the wonderful world of English and Special Needs."

Jack eyed him up and down, and then reluctantly took his hand and shook it. "Okay," he said.

Tarquin Tree put up his hand and said, "Okay if I write this like a rap?"

Jim turned to Tarquin, a skinny boy in a T-shirt with yellow and black hoops, like a bee. "You can write it any way you like, Tarquin, so long as it's original, descriptive, and doesn't rhyme 'rap' with 'crap'."

"I do a thing like that, Mr Rook? You won't never see me do a thing like that! If you ever see me rhyme rap with crap, you got my permission to give me a slap. You can slap me so hard, you can give me a hit, I won't never use no words like—"

"*Tarquin,*" said Jim, pointing his finger at him. Tarquin was instantly silent, although his hand kept flapping on the table in rap-time. Jim had told this year's class that his finger was a phaser, set to kill. He didn't point it very often, but when he did, they knew that he was serious. It meant *that's it, you've gone over the line.*

"Get here okay?" Jim asked Jack. "You're living over on La Grange, aren't you?"

9

"Pico. My dad's rented this house. I don't know how long for."

"He's working here, isn't he?"

"Finishing off a TV special, all about Alaska."

"And what happens when he's finished doing that?"

"I don't know. Maybe we'll stay, maybe we won't."

"You always follow your dad around?"

"Don't got a choice. My mom died six years ago. And traveling around, that's his work."

"You must be finding the weather a little different."

"It's okay in Anchorage, this time of year. But up in Yukon-Charley it gets pretty cold."

"Well, I hope you'll have the opportunity to tell us all about it. How much of a chance did you get to study, up in Yukon-Charley?"

Jack shrugged. "We had books to read. Like encyclopedias and stuff."

"What was the last book you read?"

"McGeary's Snowmobile Maintenance."

"Say *what?*" said Washington, with a hoot, but Jim gave him a look which meant, *remember your first day, when you had to tell me what* you'd *been reading?*

"How about novels, or poetry, or plays?"

Jack shook his head. "Only this one novel, *The Process*, about a guy who crosses the Sahara Desert and goes out of his brain."

"That sounds cool. Do you still have a copy?"

"It's probably packed up someplace, but yes, I guess."

"That's a pretty empty spot, the Sahara. Just like Yukon-Charley, I guess. Did you associate with any of the feelings in the book? I mean, the isolation, that kind of thing?"

Jack lowered his eyes and thought for a moment. Then he raised them, and said, "You're never alone, wherever you are."

Jim made a little circling gesture with his hand, to indicate that he wanted to explain himself more fully.

"You can be right out in the snow, hundreds of miles from the nearest trading-post. Nothing but white wherever you look. White, white, white, until you've got stuff dancing in front of your eyes, and you're sick of it. But you aint never alone. Never."

There was something in Jack's voice that led Jim to think that learning to deal with his isolation up in Alaska must have been one of the most critical experiences in his life so far. *White, white, white, until you're sick of it.* He hadn't heard one of his students speak so vehemently about anything for a very long time. Not since Waylon Price had gone looking for his missing sister one night, and found her in a rundown house off Melrose, dead of an overdose.

"Well," said Jack, "you've come fresh into this class today but it shouldn't take you any time to settle. Rook's First Law is that everybody in this class has to be friends and help each other, because Rook's Second Law states that nobody is stupider than anybody else, even though I have to admit that some people are really working on it. You're allowed to laugh at each other's mistakes, because that's what it's like in the real world outside of this classroom, everybody laughs at your mistakes, and that's a fact of life you're just going to have to learn to deal with."

Jack picked up his pen and said, "Do you want me to . . . describe you? Like everybody else is?"

"Sure. This is the first time you've seen me. Maybe you'll come up with something really fresh."

"Yeah, like you look like fresh shit," put in Ray Krueger, and then ducked his head down, in the hope that Jim hadn't seen him.

"Ray," said Jim, "I have a little chore for you. I want you to go to the men's room and pull out a hundred sheets of toilet tissue. I want you to write on every single one, 'This is the only place for shit.'"

"You're kidding me, Mr Rook. That's going to take me for ever."

"If you argue, I'll make it 'excrement' instead."

Ray reluctantly stood up and made his way to the classroom door, accompanied by whistles and clapping and Bronx cheers. He was a skinny boy, with bleached-blond hair that flopped around in front of his eyes. He was amazing with animals, sensitive and gentle and intuitive, and he desperately wanted to be a vet. The only trouble was, his English skills were those of an eight-year-old, and he had an alarming tendency to burst out with insults and obscenities, just at the wrong moment. Borderline Tourette's, the college psychiatrist reckoned.

Ray left the classroom. Jim went over to his desk and dropped back into his chair. He started to sort out all of the homework that he had dropped in the parking-lot.

Tarquin Tree had written, 'Hamlet goes halfway nuts because he's the only one who knows the truth about who offed his father. The only way he can get his revenge is by offing King Claudius. He offs Claudius, but he gets offed, too, on account of the swords are poisoned. So the moral is that if your mother's a fox watch out for your uncle.'

He thought: he's getting there. At least he's read the play and understood it. And even if he can't fully express himself in writing, he's had a try.

He smeared his hand over his face as if he could smooth it out and rearrange it, but it didn't make him feel any better. He probably had one or two Anacin tablets in his desk drawer, so he pulled it open to have a look. Immediately, he shouted out, "*Ah!*"

Crouched right in the front of it, right on top of his college diary, was a huge green furry rat. God, it must have gotten itself trapped in his drawer somehow, at the end of last semester, and slowly suffocated, and then rotted.

"Hey, what's the matter, Mr Rook?" asked Washington, half rising to his feet. "You look like – you look like you seen a ghost."

"It's okay, it's okay. Nobody panic." Jim picked up his mechanical pencil and gave the rat a tentative prod. "Kyle, go call Clarence, would you? Tell him to bring his protective gloves and a plastic trash bag."

It was incredible that the rat's fur had grown so long and such a poisonous shade of green. He prodded it again, and to his disgust it fell apart, revealing its whitish, semi-liquefied insides, and a membrane of transparent green slime. The smell was appalling, like overripe cheese. Then he suddenly realized that it *was* overripe cheese. This wasn't a rat at all, but a cambazola and lettuce ciabatta. He had hurriedly dropped it into his desk drawer on the last day of last semester when Karen Goudemark, the new biology teacher, had come into his classroom to introduce herself.

Like the Queen of Denmark, Karen Goudemark was a fox. Brunette, pretty, confident, with a bosom that you had to make a deliberate effort not to look at, because you were both professionals, after all. And gorgeous lips. And great ankles. You didn't greet a woman who looks like that with a messy half-eaten cheese roll in your hand.

To a chorus of exaggerated revulsion, Jim lifted the ciabatta out of his desk, balanced on his diary, and dropped it into his wastebin.

"Something sure is rotten in the state of Denmark," said Billyjo Muntz, flapping her hand in front of her nose.

"An extra credit for a spontaneous and appropriate quotation from the Bard," said Jim.

"I got one! I got one!" said Joyce Capistrano. "Act 1, scene 2 – 'the memory be green'!"

13

"Okay, an extra credit for you, too. But let's get back to work, shall we? I've got your homework to sort out."

He was just about to sit down again when Ray walked back into the classroom. He didn't have any toilet-paper, and he was frowning as if he couldn't understand what was happening to him.

"Ray?" said Jim. "Ray – is everything all right?"

Ray stared at him. "I went to the guys' room," he said.

"That's right. And?"

"And . . . I think you'd better take a look for yourself."

Two

Jim stepped out of the classroom just as Clarence came along the corridor wearing a livid red pair of industrial gloves and carrying a heavy-duty plastic bag. "What's going down now, Mr Rook? You only been back here ten minutes and already there's an emergency crisis."

"Tautology," said Jim.

"What's that? Contagious?"

"Tautology means using two words when one word will do. Like emergency crisis."

"That's right. That's exactly precisely what it is. So what's going down here?"

"I don't know yet. I thought I had a rat in my desk but it wasn't, but Ray went to the mensroom and there seems to be some kind of a problem there."

"You had a rat? Why are you walking so fast?"

"I always walk fast. It wasn't a rat, it was a cheese sandwich."

"Easy mistake to make, I guess."

"When they rot, Clarence, it isn't easy to tell the difference between a human being and a pig."

"I thought you said it was a rat."

"It wasn't. It was a cheese sandwich."

They arrived outside the door to the mensroom and stopped. Ray, who had been following close behind them, pointed to the small circular window in the middle of it.

The glass had always been frosted; but now it was covered in sparkling ice-crystals, too. Jim reached up and touched it, and his fingertip made a small melting dimple in them.

He laid his hand flat against the door. It was so cold that there was a patina of fog over it. When he took his hand away, he left a palm and fingerprints on it.

"You went inside?" he asked Ray.

Dean nodded his head wildly up and down. "You can't believe it, Mr Rook! It's like a goddamned ice-cave in there!"

Jim said, "Second time this morning."

"For what?" asked Clarence.

"Unnatural cold. The water-fountain outside Geography Four was frozen solid."

"That's impossible."

"I don't care. I saw it. And what about this? You feel this door. That's impossible, too. This is the second-hottest day of the year so far."

"What do you think it is, Mr Rook?" asked Ray. "Second Ice Age, maybe?"

"I don't have any idea," said Jim. Whatever it was, he felt so hungover that he wished it weren't happening. It was going to be enough of a struggle getting through a normal college day without an 'emergency crisis'. He pushed the mensroom door, and it opened up with a squeaking, cracking sound. Inside, there was a dense frozen fog, so that it was almost impossible to see, but he cautiously stepped forward, waving his arms from side to side to clear it. Clarence came up behind him, but Ray stayed in the doorway, reluctant to come any further.

"There's something wrong in there, Mr Rook. Like, there's a real bad smell, and it aint the usual."

With the door open, and warmer air flowing into the mensroom, the fog began to eddy away. The sight that

16

met Jim's eyes was extraordinary. The whole room was thick with ice. The washbasins were encased in it, so that they were twice their normal size, with icicles hanging down from them like sharks' teeth. The mirrors were all frozen over; and the toilets looked like nothing but huge white mushrooms. Everything glittered. Jim looked around for a moment, his breath smoking, and then he sniffed.

"Ray's right. There *is* a smell. Like dead fish."

"The drains are probably froze up," said Clarence. "Let's hope they aint burst."

Jim took two or three more awkward steps across the nubbly, ice-covered floor. "But how do you think this happened, Clarence? There isn't a refrigeration unit within five hundred feet of this room. And even if there were – well, it couldn't do this, could it?"

Clarence blew out his cheeks so that he looked like Louis Armstrong. "No, sir, it couldn't. I absolutely don't know what in heaven or earth could have done this."

Jim broke a lump of ice off the side of one of the basins. He lifted it close to his nose and smelled it. "Fish, no doubt about it. Maybe we're dealing with a disgruntled former pupil who now runs his own fish-packing business."

"Maybe we are. But how's he going to tip a truckload of ice into the mensroom without nobody seeing him do it? And how's he going to get it in here? The windows are much too small."

"Apart from that," said Jim, "what kind of revenge do you call this anyway? Freezing a john?"

Clarence tapped his shoulder. "Mr Rook. Take a look at this, Mr Rook."

Jim turned around so that he was facing the mirrors over the washbasins. All of them had begun to thaw now, so that they were obscured by nothing more than a wet, silvery haze. On every one of them, though, somebody had drawn four

17

vertical lines, each with a blob on top, so that they looked like four stick men. Jim went up to them and stared at them closely, but they were already beginning to dribble.

"I don't like this," he said. "Maybe we ought to call the cops."

"The Dean won't appreciate you doing that, Mr Rook."

"I don't care if he appreciates it or not. This is a very bizarre event we're witnessing here, Clarence. It can't be a natural phenomenon. I mean I've heard of micro-climates but you don't get the North Pole in your mensroom in the middle of June."

"So who do you think did it?"

"I don't know. But kids get up to all kinds of weird revenge things these days. Going on the rampage with guns, shooting everybody in sight. Blowing up schools. If we ignore this, who knows what might happen?"

"You're probably right, Mr Rook, but on your own head be it. Don't say I didn't never give you no warning caution."

"Everything okay in there, Mr Rook?" called Ray.

"Fine so far. We'll be out in a minute."

Jim circled the room. On the right-hand side, a college sweatshirt was hanging on a peg, and it was frozen so hard that he could have used it for a surfboard. He pushed open the doors to the toilet cubicles. In the corner of the last cubicle, there was a thick accretion of white ice, although it was already beginning to melt, and become more transparent. Jim was about to turn away when he thought he saw a faint dark shape inside the ice. Maybe it was just a shadow; or the toilet-brush holder caught in the ice. But he peered again more closely, and rubbed the heel of his hand across the surface of the ice to clear away the rime.

There was something trapped inside there, no question about it. He could distinguish a small head, with pointed ears, and a body, and four legs. It was an animal – a black cat, by the look of it – caught by the ice in mid-air, as it tried to jump up onto the toilet-seat.

"Clarence, come here. Looks like we've got ourselves a deep-frozen moggy."

Clarence hunkered down and gave the ice another rub. "Jeez, I know that cat. It's been prowling around here for the past few days. I tried to shoo it away but it wouldn't go."

"Well, it's sure stuck here now."

"You're not kidding. Think how quick it must have froze in here, to catch it like that. Even its goddamn eyes are still open."

"Couldn't have felt a thing," said Jim.

At that moment Ray came up behind them. "Mr Rook – Dr Friendly's coming down the hall."

"Okay, thanks for the warning caution. Did you ever seen anything like this before?"

Ray leaned forward and stared at the block of rapidly dissolving ice. "Hey – that's a cat in there!"

"That's right. It got caught. The temperature must have dropped in a fraction of a second."

"We ought to break it out of there."

"What's the point? It won't be long before the ice has all melted."

"No, but I was reading about this before, in one of my animal magazines. A husky fell through the ice someplace up north, Greenland, someplace like that. It was frozen solid in five minutes flat, and they thought it was dead. But they slowly warmed it up and brought it back to life. Like, it had gone into suspended animation."

Jim was impressed. "I wish you read Shakespeare with as much enthusiasm as you read *Dogs Daily*."

"Come on, we should get it out of there quick," urged Ray. "Even a few seconds can make all the difference."

19

Clarence took a heavy wrench out of his tool-belt. "This should do it," he said. Jim hefted it in his hand, then swung it right back and cracked it down on top of the ice. Small chips flew everywhere, but the wrench made hardly any impression.

Ray said, "Look – it's all melted underneath. We should be able to lift it up and drop it."

"Okay," said Jim. "But don't strain your back. The college isn't insured for injuries caused by frozen cats."

Between the three of them, they managed to wrestle the block of ice out of the corner behind the toilet pedestal and into the center of the cubicle. It was roughly pyramid-shaped, and it must have weighed more than eighty-five pounds. All the same, they knelt down, gripped the block underneath, and managed to lift it up clear of the toilet seat. Jim could see the cat staring at him through the ice, its yellow eyes unblinking, its mouth slightly open so that its teeth were bared in a silent yowl of surprise.

"Okay now," he said. "Lift it up as high as you can . . . that's it . . . and when I count to three, drop it on the floor."

They heaved the dripping block over their heads. Ice-melt ran down their wrists and into their sleeves. "Higher," Jim urged them. Then, "One, two, three – drop it!"

The block dropped to the floor and cracked in half. The cat flopped out of it, lifeless and bedraggled. Jim lifted its head. Its eyes were still open but there was no doubt that it was dead. "I'm sorry," said Jim. "It couldn't have survived being frozen like that."

But Ray said, "No, no, there's a chance!" He picked up the cat's dangling body and held it close to his chest. "I'll take it outside, where it's warm."

He was carrying the cat toward the door when Dr Friendly walked in. Dr Friendly looked around at the rapidly melting ice and his mouth opened and stayed open. Then, after a while, he looked down at the water pouring over his gray suede shoes and said, "What the *hell* is happening in here?"

Ray ducked around behind him, and Jim heard his Nikes slapping away along the corridor.

"Little technical problem, sir," said Clarence, standing up, and returning his wrench to his tool-belt.

"Little *technical* problem?" Dr Friendly echoed, walking up to one of the washbasins, which was still thick with ice and noisily dripping icicles. "I might have known you were part of this, Mr Rook. Little *technical* problem? This looks like subversion to me. This looks like sabotage.

He walked right up to Jim and stared at him from such close range that he made Jim feel like a waxwork. "What kind of a little *technical* problem causes something like this? Ice, everywhere. *Ice!* This is deliberate."

Jim couldn't do anything but shrug. "Maybe it is. I don't know. But if it is deliberate, how was it done?"

"Oh, somebody found a way of doing it. One of those snow-blowing machines they use in the movies, that's what they used. Rented one, probably."

"Well, it's a theory. But why?"

"*Why?*"

"Yes, why? Why rent a snow-blowing machine for the sole purpose of turning a college restroom into an igloo?"

The muscles around the corners of Dr Friendly's mouth worked as furiously as if he were trying to chew a particularly nasty piece of gristle. "Students . . . you can't work out what's going on inside of their heads. They're not logical. They're not rational. You're a college teacher, how can you ask me *why*? There is no *why*! Ask them! Ask your students! They don't know why they ever do anything! You know what the job of a college teacher is? To turn complete and utter cretins into something that can walk on two legs and add up its grocery bill. To take those self-centered, self-indulgent, sweaty, spotty young geeks, and turn them through knowledge and discipline into remotely acceptable members of the human race – people who can read a newspaper the right way up and cross the road without being mown down by the first bus that comes along.

"But they fight us. They fight us every inch of the way. They defend their stupidity like the Alamo. And this—" he said, waving his arm at the ice-covered basins "—this is the kind of thing they do, to stop us from civilizing them. And they think it's clever. They think this is hilarious! The day we froze the mensroom! What a killer!"

Jim said, "This wasn't students."

"So who was it?"

"I don't know. But it wasn't students. Students pull some pretty ridiculous stunts, I'll admit. It's their job. But there isn't any point to this at all."

Dr Friendly stared at him for a long time, the breath fuming out of his nostrils. "So what are you saying? That it was a natural phenomenon? A miracle? An act of God?"

"I don't know. I think we ought to keep an open mind. I also think we ought to call the police."

"Absolutely not. We've had enough trouble on this campus already, and we're only a week into the new semester. That commissary riot, that was enough. Fettucine everywhere. Besides, this is all going to melt by the time the police get here, and then what are we going to say? 'Some drug-crazed vandal made our washroom all wet'?"

Jim said, "I'm only going on intuition, sir. But I have a

very bad feeling about this."

"Yes, Mr Rook, I've heard all about your psychic sensitivity. Maybe hysteria's a better word for it. I don't know what caused this freezing, but it's melting now, and that's all I care about. The best thing we can do is ignore it."

"Let me tell you something, sir. The temperature in this room must have plunged down to minus fifty degrees Celsius, maybe lower, all in the blink of an eye. And you're telling me to ignore it?"

"Exactly. If it's a prank, the best thing that we can do is show no interest in it whatsoever. If it's a meteorological phenomenon, we can't do anything about it anyhow. So the best plan is simply to tell yourself that you were dreaming: that it never happened. Then we can all get on with the business of running a college without worrying about things that are never going to be satisfactorily explained, whatever we do."

"And if it happens again?"

"It won't happen again."

"But if it does?"

"Read my lips, Mr Rook. It's not going to happen again because it didn't happen this time, either. I expressly forbid you to mention this incident ever again, to anyone, and that includes the police and the Press."

"A cat got killed this time around. What if a student gets frozen to death? What are you going to say about that?"

"I told you, Mr Rook, loud and clear. It won't happen again."

Jim stared at Dr Friendly for a long, long time before he finally took his eyes away. "I hope you're willing to lay money on that," he remarked.

"I'm not a betting man, Mr Rook."

"I'll bet you're not."

*   *   *

Jim found Ray on the sloping lawns outside, with the cat wrapped up in a West Grove college sweatshirt. He was doggedly massaging the cat's heart with his fingertips, but the cat's head was lolling back over his knee with its lip exposed in a deathly snarl.

"Ray, come on, man. Why don't you give it up? There isn't a creature alive which could have survived that."

"How about cockroaches?" suggested Christophe l'Ouverture – a very stylish Haitian boy who wore some of the most expensive clothes in the class. He had dreadlocks and flappy white pants and a yellow silk shirt from Armani, the color of molten gold. He bared his white teeth. "Cockroaches can survive any destructive force known to man. Insecticides, H-bombs, earthquakes, floods."

"This isn't a cockroach, this is a cat," said Ray. "And I read about it. Cats can survive extreme temperatures. Somebody cooked a cat in a bread-oven once, and it survived. Kind of crispy, sure. But it was still alive."

Jim peered at the cat and said, "It's dead. No doubt about it."

"I could give it the kiss of life," Ray suggested.

"What?" Christophe exploded. "You're going to kiss a dead cat? That's so sick! Uggh! Fwah! You pervert! You must be out of your ever-living mind!"

But Ray didn't hesitate. He pressed his thumb over the cat's nostrils, took a deep breath, and clamped his lips around its mouth.

"Go easy," Jim warned him. "Just remember how much smaller its lungs are. You could burst them if you blow too hard."

Ray lifted his head and took another breath. "It's been eating tuna," he remarked, before he bent down to blow into its lungs for a second time.

He dipped his head down again and again, and kept on massaging the animal's heart, but after five minutes there was still no sign of life.

"Ray," said Jim, laying a hand on his shoulder. "I know you want to be a vet. I know you want to save animals' lives. But this one, I'm sorry. This one is really beyond saving."

Just then Laura Killmeyer came walking across the grass, followed as usual by Dottie Osias. Laura was petite and thin, with long shining black hair and a face as white as chalk, with big black eyes and spidery eyelashes. She was wearing a headband of silver coins and a short dress of red chiffon with gold and silver moons printed on it, and sandals that laced right up to her knee. She was one of the prettiest girls in the class, or she would have been if she hadn't insisted on making herself up to look like the Wicked Witch of the West. Dottie was plump and fair with frizzy hair and hot red cheeks, and today she was wearing a large beige tracksuit. But she showed her devotion to Laura's mysticism by wearing a large silver pentacle around her neck.

"What's happening, Mr Rook?" asked Laura, touching him on the shoulder. She was always touching him, only gently, not suggestively. She believed that touching was the way in which fellow souls communicated, and that words were irrelevant. On her first day in Jim's class, she had offered to stroke his forehead for five minutes instead of writing a critical essay on *The Raven* by Edgar Allan Poe. He had, of course, declined.

Dottie adored Laura because Laura was fiercely protective of her, and never criticized her incredible clumsiness, nor her asthma, nor her failure to attract any boyfriends; and because she allowed her to share the secrets of her amateur witchcraft. Jim seriously believed that Dottie would have died for Laura, if she had ever asked her. Yet when it came to English, it was Dottie who had a far deeper understanding of words, and what they meant, and she was often moved to tears by poetry that left Laura completely baffled.

Jim stood up. "We found a dead cat in the washroom, that's all. Ray's been trying to revive it."

Laura knelt down next to Ray and stroked the cat's fur. "It's not dead," she said.

"I'm sorry, Laura, it's not breathing. That counts for dead in my book."

"Ah, but your book isn't my book. My book says that when you're dead, your spirit leaves you, and hurries away. But this cat's spirit hasn't left yet. This cat's spirit is only hiding. And all we have to do is look into his eyes like this—"

Here she took hold of the cat's head in the palm of her hand and bent forward so that she was staring at it from less than six inches away. The cat stared back at her, yellow-eyed, but still dead – as far as Jim was concerned, anyhow.

"—and we search for its spirit, which is hiding someplace inside of its body. We rummage around with our eyes. We look through its brain, and its lungs, and its liver. Its spirit hasn't gone yet. It's only hiding, because it's mortally afraid. It won't come out. And – *look* – here it is, hiding in its heart. Stiff with fear. Paralyzed. Which is why its heart stopped. If people only realized that."

Ray looked up at Jim, and it was obvious by the expression on his face that all of this mumbo-jumbo made him feel deeply uncomfortable, especially since he had tried so hard to save the cat's life. Jim gave him a little dismissive shake of his head, as if to say, 'Let her try. She can't do it any harm.'

Laura pressed her forehead between the cat's ears and murmured to it, crooned to it, very softly. Jim could catch only a little of what she was singing. ". . . *don't hide yourself*

*. . . come out, we pray . . . come out and dance in the light of
day . . . in the rabbinical book it saith . . . the cats cry when,
with icy breath . . . Great Sammael, the Angel of Death . . .
takes through the town his flight . . ."*

"Laura, it's bought the farm," Ray protested. "Don't mess
with it any more. Give it some dignity."

But Laura raised her hand over the cat's body and wrote
a figure in the air. Nobody could have realized what it was,
except for Jim, because he was able to see things that other
people couldn't see. He could see shadows, spirits, and
ghosts. And he could by the lingering disturbance that Laura
had left in the air that she had drawn a curl with a tail.

"What's that?" he asked her, nodding toward the shape
in the air as if it were still there.

"A ghost-mouse," she said. "It's one of the things that
cats can't resist."

"What's a ghost-mouse?"

"It's a little part of your soul. When you sleep – especially
if you sleep with your mouth open – a bright little ghost-
mouse escapes through your lips and runs around the house.
Nothing can stop it and nobody knows what it wants. But if
you wake up before the ghost-mouse returns, you lose a little
part of your soul. That's why you should never let a cat stay
in the room with you while you sleep. It will always try
to catch your ghost-mouse as it comes out of your mouth.
That's why there are far more unexplained deaths in households with cats than there are in households without them."

"Ghost-mouse, huh?" said Jim. "Well, you learn something new every day."

"You can see spirits and stuff, can't you, sir? You should
be able to see ghost-mice, too."

She drew the figure again, and then again, and softly
called out, "Come on, cat. Come on back. I know you're
only hiding."

"Come on, Laura," said Ray. "Leave it alone, it's history. Don't you think I tried everything?"

But Laura closed her eyes and tilted her head back so that the sun shone from the coins around her hair. She whispered something that Jim couldn't hear, but he suspected what it was. The revival. The invocation to the dead, to return. He felt the back of his neck prickle.

She stood up. The cat lay on the grass, its legs wide apart, its dried-out fur fluffing in the breeze.

"What did I tell you? Dead!"

But then it seemed as if a cold shiver swept across the grass, like a cloud briefly covering the sun. Jim looked up, and when he looked back, the cat had lifted its head and was looking at him.

"It's alive!" squealed Dottie. "Look, Mr Rook! It's alive!"

Slowly, the cat rolled itself over. It lay on its side for a while, panting. Then, on trembling legs, it managed to stand up. Laura knelt down beside it again, and held out her hand, and the cat suspiciously sniffed at the tips of her fingers.

"I can't believe it," said Ray. "I could have sworn it was totally and utterly kaput."

"Me too," Jim told him. "I know cats are supposed to have nine lives, but that was pushing it."

The cat walked around in a cautious circle, sniffing and peering at all of them. Eventually it walked over to Jim and rubbed itself against his legs.

"Looks like you've been adopted, Mr Rook," said Christophe.

"Unh-hunh. Not me. I've been planning on buying a dog."

"Too late now. She's definitely taken a shine to you."

Jim picked the cat up and stroked her. He didn't believe in fate, as a rule, but ever since he had lost his previous cat, the

28

feline formerly known as Tibbles, he had felt that he would show up again, somehow, maybe in a different form. And he could hardly ignore the spectacular way in which this cat had appeared.

"What are you going to call her?" asked Dottie, tickling her.

"I don't know. Maybe Mrs Horowitz. My old grade-school teacher was called Mrs Horowitz, and she always looked as if somebody had just miraculously brought her back from the dead."

"You should never give a cat a human name," said Laura. "Like you should never let it share anything personal with you, especially your food. Cats are very vulnerable to demonic possession, especially if you treat them as equals. Why do you think witches use them as familiars?"

"You really believe that?" asked Jim.

"Sure I do. You shouldn't laugh at myths and stories and old wives' tales. There's always a grain of truth in them somewhere."

"Okay, then. I won't call her Mrs Horowitz. We don't want to have to call in the pet exorcist, do we?"

"Why don't you call her Titanic?" said Christophe. "She was just like the ship, right? She had a fatal encounter with a large block of ice."

"You can't call a cat Titanic."

"You can call a cat anything you like. My mother had a cat called Ropa Vieja because she found him in a basket of old clothes."

"I think you should call her Popsicle," Dottie suggested. "How about Tastee-Freez?"

Jim said, "I think I'll stick to Tibbles."

"Tibbles Two: The Return!" announced Ray, dramatically.

Jim let the cat jump onto the ground. It walked off a little way, and then stopped and waited for him.

"I think you're being summoned," smiled Laura, one hand raised against the sunlight.

Three

Before he went home that night, Jim went up to the college library and searched through books on ice and snow and natural disasters.

He found several instances of sudden cold snaps. In 1921, at Silver Lake, Colorado, 87 inches of snow fell in 27½ hours. And he found at least four different incidents in which people and animals had been encased in ice.

In 1930, five German glider pilots had been carried into a thundercloud over the Rhön Mountains, and had parachuted out of their aircraft. They had been swept upward into regions of supercooled vapor, and had become the nuclei for five giant hailstones. They dropped to the ground and only one of them survived.

In Candle, Alaska, in February 1948, the temperature had dropped so abruptly that a party of seven petro-chemical engineers were covered in a thick coating of ice and frozen where they stood, like statues.

But Jim couldn't find any record of ice forming in isolated pockets during warm weather, the way it had in the mensroom. He came across two or three stories on the Internet about haunted houses, in which some of the rooms were unnaturally chilly. However, it was a long way from 'unnaturally chilly' to 'frozen solid'.

All the time he sat in the library, Tibbles Two sat on a chair not far away, watching him intently, as if she were making sure that he wasn't going to run off and leave her behind.

On his way back to his car, with Tibbles Two walking close behind him, he saw Jack Hubbard sitting on the tail of his bright yellow Dodge pick-up talking to Linda Starewsky. Linda was a tall, intense girl, all arms and legs, with curly red hair that bounced all around her head like rusty springs. She came from a family who took education very seriously. In fact, they took everything very seriously, and always wore suits and neckties whenever they came to the college to discuss Linda's future. Mack Petrie, the physics teacher, called them 'The Funeral Party'. Linda's problem was that she found it extremely difficult to distinguish between different word-shapes. Even the word 'word' could be 'draw' or 'road' as far as she was concerned. Her lack of confidence had led to her becoming chronically anorexic, and Jim was aware that if he could teach her to read properly, he might also save her life.

"Well," said Jim, throwing his evening's marking into the back seat of his Cadillac. "What did you think about your first day?"

"I was just talking to Linda about it," said Jack, shielding his eyes against the six o'clock sun. "It wasn't anything like I was expecting it to be. I thought it was going to be all dusty old stuff like Longfellow, you know?"

"I do Longfellow," said Jim. "'But the father answered never a word . . . a frozen corpse was he.'"

"That's pretty appropriate, considering what happened in the john today."

"How about, 'A traveler, by the faithful hound . . . half-buried in the snow was found.'"

"Jack's been telling me about snow," said Linda, grinning and showing her glittering silver brace. "He says that it's not true that the Inuit have twenty-three different names for snow. And he says that you can tell what the temperature is, by the noise the snow makes when you walk on it."

"That true?" asked Jim.

Jack nodded. "If you tread on snow and it gives out a deep crunch, that means it's only just below zero degrees C. At minus five the pitch rises and the snow makes a creaking noise that's kind of higher up the scale. At minus fifteen it sounds like the highest violin notes you ever heard, being played real bad. Lower than that, and it's almost unbearable. Like a knife being scraped on a dinner-plate."

"Handy to know," said Jim. He turned and watched as Tibbles Two jumped into the back of his car and sat primly next to his sheaf of homework.

Jack said, "Not much use in LA. But up past the Arctic Circle . . . well, it can make all the difference between living and dying."

"You don't have any theories about what happened today, do you?" asked Jim.

Jack shook his head. "It was just weird, wasn't it? Maybe you ought to talk to my old man. He's the expert on snow and ice. You ought to see some of the video footage he took up at the Arctic National Wildlife Refuge. Now that was awesome. He got caught in this Arctic blizzard and he almost didn't make it."

"Well, sure, I'd be very interested to meet him. Tell him to drop by the college some day, after class."

"I'll sure try."

Just then, Karen Goudemark came past, accompanied by two other faculty members, Roger Persky from the biology department and Chuck Rolle, the phys-ed instructor. Roger wore hugely magnifying glasses and a brown-and-white seersucker sport coat. Chuck had a face like a pork knuckle and a white T-shirt full of various assorted muscles. Both of them were walking possessively close to her, and when Jim gave her a wave they crowded even closer still.

"Jim!" called Karen. "I hear you found yourself a new cat today!" God, she was gorgeous. She was wearing a lemon short-sleeved sweater and a straight white skirt and she looked as if she had just finished serving ice-creams in Heaven.

"That's right, do you want to meet her?"

Roger Persky checked his watch as if to say, you don't have time to meet Jim Rook's cat, for goodness' sake; and Chuck Rolle arched his back and flexed his arms and looked at Jim as if he were working out how hard he would have to hit him, should the need arise.

Karen came over and Jim took hold of her arm and led her to his car. "There . . . what do you think of her? Incredible to think she was stuck in a block of ice. Cute, isn't she?"

But Tibbles Two instantly scrabbled to her feet and let out a harsh, spiteful hiss. The fur on her back stood up and her tail turned into a bottle-brush. Karen reached out to stroke her and she retreated, her claws snagging on the leather seat and her head flattening like a cobra.

"She sure doesn't like me," said Karen.

"She sees you as competition, that's all."

"Competition? Competition for what?"

"Well, you know, competition for me. For my affections. Female cats are like that. They don't realize they're cats. So every time an attractive woman walks into their owner's life, they naturally get a little spiky about it. And – well, that's you. An attractive woman."

Karen looked at Jim with slightly narrowed eyes but she didn't say anything. After a perceptibly long moment, Roger Persky took hold of her elbow and said, "We'd better get moving, if we want to miss the worst of the traffic."

"Roger's – ah – giving you a ride home?" asked Jim

"Roger's taking me out for a drink. Well, Roger *and* Chuck."

"That's great. That's really great."

"But what?"

"I didn't say but. I never mentioned the word but."

"You didn't have to. I could see it in your eyes."

"I have buts in my eyes?"

"Really, Karen," Roger fretted. "We ought to be making a move."

"I was just thinking that you're one up on Olive Oyl," said Jim. "Even she never got to date Popeye *and* Bluto, both at the same time."

Chuck stabbed a finger into Jim's chest. "Do you know something, Jim? You can be a very offensive person sometimes."

"It was a joke, Chuck. Only a joke. I hope you three have a great, great time. Are you going on anyplace afterward? A disco? You should get them to take you to a disco, Karen. Roger is the West Coast watusi champion. Chuck can't dance but he can flex his muscles in time to the music."

Karen smiled and shook her head but she didn't laugh. The three of went off leaving Jim standing by his car. He punched his fist so hard against the side of the door that he almost broke his fingers. Jack and Linda saw him, and he had to grin and give them the thumbs-up, even though it hurt so much he could have exhausted every foul word in his vocabulary. He climbed into his car and started up the engine with a deep, chesty whoosh, followed by a deafening backfire. He couldn't believe himself sometimes. He could just see himself standing there with a gooey look on his face, saying: 'And well – that's you, an attractive woman.' And that insane remark about Popeye and Bluto. He was so embarrassed that he when he stopped at the college gates he banged his forehead two or three times on the steering-wheel. What was Karen going to think of him now? A leering idiot with all the sophisticated come-on technique of a Kansas-based toupée salesman.

At the intersection with Santa Monica Boulevard a new blue Cougar drew up beside him with a sun-tanned young woman in it, its stereo throbbing with rock music. Usually he would have leaned back nonchalantly in his seat and taken off his sunglasses and given her one of his worldly Jack Nicholson expressions. But this evening he stayed crunched behind the wheel, with a bright red mark across his forehead, feeling about thirteen years old. His new apartment was on the top floor of a white block on Windward Avenue. It had been built in 1911 in the Italianate style, and even though it had suffered from some crass remodeling in the early 1960s, it had still had an elegance and a coolness about it which was hard to find, even in Venice.

It had a large living-room with high ceilings and a window overlooking the courtyard in the center of the block. Outside the window there was a narrow balcony that was just about wide enough to accommodate two basketwork chairs and a broken Mexican drum which Jim used as an occasional table.

At the far end of the living-room there was a dining area with a brown Formica-topped table and a hatch through to the kitchen. There were two bedrooms – although one of them was so small that you had to climb on the bed to get in and out of the door.

Jim had tried to decorate it more stylishly than his last place. He had bought three large abstract paintings of red circles and a green and blue composition that looked like a Christmas tree toppling off a mailbox. He had arranged some blue-dyed pampas grass in a tall earthenware vase, and he had found the papier-mâché effigy of a horse under the stage at college. It was bright yellow with staring eyes which followed him around the room but he thought it looked cheerful.

Tibbles Two followed him cautiously into the apartment, and proceeded to have a comprehensive sniff at everything. He went into the kitchen and unpacked his shopping. He had remembered what Laura Killmeyer had told him about feeding your cat on human food, and he had stopped at Ralph's on the way home and bought seven cans of turkey'n'gravy; as well two chicken breasts and a quarter of Fontina cheese for himself, so that he could cook his favorite hangover dish of chicken and melted cheese and volcanically hot salsa.

He popped the top of a can of Coors and took six long swallows, which was two too many because he had to stand in the kitchen for almost a minute with his eyes watering, punching himself in the chest to bring up the wind. Then he took his beer out on to the balcony to enjoy the last warmth of the day, and the ocean breeze that blew inshore at this time of day. Tibbles Two came out to join him, and hopped up on to the other chair as if she had lived with him all her life.

"So where did you come from?" he asked her. "From what benighted shore were you washed up?"

Tibbles Two stared at him through slitted eyes. Jim had often wondered whether it would be possible to discover what cats were thinking. Maybe you could monitor their synaptic impulses and turn them into computer images. Mind you, the result would probably be nothing more than a kaledeiscopic jumble of fish-heads and warm cushions and sudden lunatic urges to chase after balls of wool.

"I hope you realize I expect total obedience out of my cats," said Jim. "You go out when I tell you and you

37

come back in when I tell you. No scratching at the door for wee-wees in the middle of the night. And when I bring girls back, you don't sit on the couch giving me death stares."

Tibbles Two thought about that for a while, and then suddenly jumped down from the chair and went into the living-room. Then she came back and stood in the open door and mewed at him.

"What do you want now? You can't be hungry. Can't you sit and relax for five minutes?"

She mewed again, and kept on mewing, and in the end he had to get up and follow her into the apartment. "You want to go to the bathroom? I hope you realize I don't like kitty litter. There is nothing guaranteed to put off a desirable woman more than a trayful of cat turds under the bathroom basin. You want to do ah-ahs, you find someplace outside."

But Tibbles Two didn't go toward the front door. Instead, she jumped up onto the back of the couch and stepped onto the small table behind it, where there was a glass-based lamp, a stack of paperback books, a seashell that his fellow teacher Bill Babouris had brought him back from Greece, and a deck of Tarot cards.

Tibbles Two stood on the table sniffing at the Tarot cards and mewing again and again.

Jim said, "This is ridiculous. You want me to tell your fortune?" But Tibbles Two stared at him intently, and he said, "I see. You want me to tell my own fortune. Well, sorry. I'm not in the mood. My fortune is that I will never get to date Karen Goudemark. Every time I see her I will say something totally dumb and she will end up thinking that I'm some kind of emotional retard. Apart from that, Dr Friendly will find a way of closing down Special Class Two and I will find myself selling pencils for a living."

He turned to go back to the balcony but Tibbles Two let out a long yowl, almost as if she had been attacked by a passing tom. She stood with one paw on top of the Tarot pack, her ears flattened and her fur bristling.

"What the hell is the matter with you?" Jim demanded. "You're a cat, get it? You don't understand what Tarot cards are. You don't even understand what the future is, let alone the fact that you can predict what it's going to be. Just get down from the table and start behaving like a normal cat. I don't know, go lick your ass or something."

But Tibbles Two stayed where she was, her fur still electric. Jim hesitated for a moment, and then he went across to the table and tugged the deck of cards from under her paw. He sat down on the couch, tipped the cards out, and proceeded to shuffle them with all the high-speed expertise of somebody who has spent many a long night losing his salary at poker. Tibbles Two dropped down on to the couch next to him and sat at his elbow, watching him acutely.

"If I find out that something really lousy is going to happen to me, I'm going to blame you for it," Jim told her. "I've had enough trouble for one day, what with that washroom turning into an iceberg, and Dr Friendly always getting on my case."

He laid the cards out in the Celtic cross pattern. He didn't often consult the Tarot these days, except when entertaining women: they were always fascinated by having their fortunes told. He found its predictions too accurate, and he preferred the disasters in his life to take him by surprise. He was always worried, too, that one day he might turn up the Death card. If he was going to be killed in an auto wreck or drop dead of a coronary occulusion he didn't want to know about it beforehand. He had learned that destiny is unavoidable, no matter what precautions you take. If the

Tarot says you're going to die, you can stay indoors and wrap yourself up in a comforter, but one way or another you're still going to die.

This evening his cards turned out to be fairly ho-hum. He was going to go to work tomorrow as usual. He was going to have a minor but irritating argument with somebody who was close to him – Dr Friendly, no doubt. He was going to be affected by an unexpected change in the weather. He was going to receive an invitation to visit somebody he had never met before – that could be interesting. And there was something that he couldn't quite understand about hands. There was definitely a combination of snapping or breaking and hands, but it was unclear what exactly it was and who it was going to happen to. It didn't appear to be him. Maybe somebody he knew was going to break a finger.

"What do you think this is all about, TT?" he asked Tibbles Two, but Tibbles Two impassively closed her eyes and didn't even mew.

He reached the second-to-last card. *This covers you* – the card that tells you what your present circumstances are, and why you need to know what your future holds for you. He picked it up and frowned at it in complete bafflement. It was a Tarot card he had never seen before. A completely new, different card. It showed a figure standing in an icy wasteland, under a black starry sky. The figure was dressed in a hooded white robe, which was rippling in the wind. Its face was completely blank, totally white, except for a pair of dark glasses with tiny, rectangular lenses. It carried a long white staff.

There were footprints in the snow beside the figure, but they were obviously the footprints of somebody who had walked close by. The figure itself had left no footprints at all.

At the foot of all the other Tarot cards, there was a

name, such as The Fool, or Death, or the Five of Wands. This card had a space for a name, but it was blank, just like the figure's face.

Jim scrutinized the card for a very long time, while Tibbles Two watched him. He had been casting Tarot cards for years, and he thought he knew the whole pack back-to-front. So where had this card come from? It couldn't have been accidentally stuck in the carton for all of this time. Even if it had been, how had it suddenly been dislodged?

There was nothing in the picture to reveal what the card might signify. The figure was simply standing in the snow, motionless. The stars had been very carefully drawn, so if he could discover what stars they were, maybe that would give him a clue.

The card gave Jim an uneasy sense of foreboding. It wasn't just the fact that he had never seen it before, but the way the figure was standing, as if it were waiting for somebody, and wouldn't leave until it got what it wanted. *Ever.*

He put the card down on the coffee table and went across to his bookshelf. He picked out his dog-eared copy of *The Tarot Interpreted* and thumbed through to the section where all the cards were illustrated in color. The Tarot deck traditionally included twenty-two trump or 'triumph' cards known as the major arcana, numbered zero to twenty-one, except for number thirteen, the Death card. Among the major arcana were the Sun, the Hanged Man, the Lovers, the Moon and the Fool. In some decks, Death was unnamed, but the card with the hooded figure on it wasn't Death. It was something else: something beyond Death. Something that stood in the frozen wilderness and waited – but God alone knew what it was waiting for.

Jim heard a sudden scuffling sound. He looked around, and saw that Tibbles Two was standing up on the couch, her eyes wide, her back arched, her teeth bared into a snarl. On top of the coffee table, the Tarot cards were dancing in the air, flying around as if they had all been caught in a gale. They whirled higher and higher off the table, going around and around, until they formed four columns of flickering, flackering pasteboard, all light and color and dazzling images.

The four columns leaned slightly to the right, almost as if they were four men leaning against the wind. Jim slowly approached them, watching them in fascination. They looked just like the four vertical lines that had been drawn on the misted-over mirrors in the college bathroom. They made a noise that reminded him of something he used to do as a boy: stick a stiff square of cardboard into his bicycle wheel, so that it made a loud clattering sound as he pedaled along.

He lifted his hand over them, but he could feel no updraft whatsoever. These cards were dancing by themselves, unblown by any natural wind.

"What the hell is this, TT?" he asked Tibbles Two. He had experienced many supernatural events before, and he was a believer. But this was extraordinary. Nearly forty fortune-telling cards were spinning around in front of his eyes, in a room without the hint of a draft, and they were showing no signs of dropping or falling or losing their momentum.

Jim knelt on the rug beside the coffee-table. He reached up and touched one of the columns of cards. Three or four of them were scattered for a moment, but then they flew back up to where they had been before. After a while, the remainder of the pack flew up into the air, as if somebody had thrown them up in the palm of their hand, and suddenly burst into thousands of tiny fragments. The pieces flew everywhere – all across the table, all across the floor, a blizzard of cardboard – while the four columns of cards bent themselves even more doggedly against an imaginary storm.

TT mewed and lifted her paw as if to say *Look, dummy. Look what's happening on your coffee table. This is a message. This is a sign. Look at what I'm showing you, and learn.*

"I don't know!" Jim shouted at her. "I don't know what the hell I'm supposed to be looking at!"

The cards whirled around faster and faster; and the snowstorm of fragments blew around the entire living-room, and even out of the window, on to the balcony, like confetti. Then, just as abruptly as they had started to dance, the cards dropped on to the table, and lay there, lifeless and scattered, while the snowstorm gradually subsided, and all of the pieces spiraled to the floor.

"Very enlightening, I don't think," said Jim, looking around his paper-strewn living-room. "Also very messy." Tibbles Two jumped down from the couch and went into the kitchen, where he could hear her noisily lapping up her soya milk. He stood up and collected all the remaining Tarot cards. He checked them all, thumbing through the whole deck three times over, but there was no sign of the card with the hooded figure on it. Must have been one of the cards that self-destructed, and turned his living-room into Santa's grotto. He followed Tibbles Two into the kitchen and dropped the rest of the deck into the trash.

He was just about to take a shower when the doorbell rang. He peered through the spyhole and saw a grossly distorted version of Mervyn Brookfeller, who lived across the hallway. He opened the door and said, "Hi, Mervyn. I was going to take a shower. Then I was going to come over and thank you for cleaning up my apartment. You did a fantastic job."

Mervyn was six feet three inches and wore platform soles which made him look even taller. He also sported an immense golden quiff which probably took him over six feet five. He wore a white satin vest embroidered with poppies and tight white satin pedal-pushers. His nails were as long as a woman's, and immaculately painted with purple polish. Although he was only a tenant like everybody else in Jim's apartment block, he had somehow appointed himself unofficial super, fixing everybody's fuses, levering the teaspoons out of their sink disposal units, keeping the hallways hoovered and listening to everybody's problems. He sang in cabaret at The Slant Club on Abbot Kinney Boulevard, under the name of Chet Sideways.

He stalked into Jim's apartment and looked around at all the ripped-up fragments of card. Then he turned to Jim with his arms held out wide, wordlessly seeking an explanation.

Jim said, "I'm sorry. You did a terrific job, really. But when I got home, there was kind of an event."

"An event? It looks like you got married. Congratulations. Who's the lucky girl?"

Tibbles Two came out of the kitchen licking her whiskers.

"You married a cat! How different! I mean, most men are always hankering after a little pussy . . . but you had the nerve to make it legal!"

"Shut up, Mervyn," said Jim. "Something happened here . . . something weird."

"In that case you'd better pour me a stiff drink."

Jim poured him out a large glassful of Jack Daniel's. He took a mouthful and shuddered, as if a goose had walked over his grave. "That hit the spot! So tell me what's been happening here."

"I don't know . . . but I feel like somebody's trying

44

to tell me something." He told Melvyn all about the frozen drinking fountain and the iced-up washroom and the dancing Tarot cards.

"You're being warned," said Melvyn, emphatically. "There's no question about it. You're being warned from beyond. My Aunt Minnie kept seeing toads in her yard, and the next thing she knew she met my Uncle Irvine. And my brother Aaron had a sign. His electric kettle shorted out, and left a burn mark on his kitchen wall in the shape of a bearded man. The next day he went out and he was run over by a bearded man in a Buick Electra."

"And?"

"And what? He died. He was only twenty-three."

"Are you kidding me?"

"That was my brother, Jim. Do you want me to show you a picture of him?"

"No, don't worry."

"But he had a warning, just like you're having a warning now. Very low temperatures, that's always a sign of impending evil. Didn't you ever see *The Exorcist*? And things that whirl around, all on their own. Very bad news. And all that ripped-up paper, looking like snow."

Yes, thought Jim. That was exactly what it looked like. Snow. Four figures toiling through a snowstorm. Somebody was trying to tell him something about cold and ice and snow; and somebody was trying to warn him that something terrible was going to happen to him.

Mervyn flitted around, picking up little pieces of playing card. He bobbed down by the coffee-table, where there was only one card left, face-down, the card which Jim hadn't had the time to turn over. *That which crosses you* – that which stands in your way.

"Don't touch that!" said Jim, as Mervyn bent forward to pick it up, but it was already too late.

"This is a bit grim, isn't it?" said Mervyn, waving the Death card between his manicured fingertips.

Four

The next morning started hot and hazy. The sky over Los Angeles was a weird, unearthly bronze, as if God were using a strawberry filter.

At first, Jim was worried that TT might want to come to college with him; but after breakfast she curled up on her chair on the balcony and fell asleep, so she was obviously quite content to stay where she was.

As he stepped out of the elevator he bumped into Mervyn. Mervyn was wearing a woman's satin robe with black-and-green Japanese flowers splashed all over it. He had been out to the corner store to buy himself a huge bottle of papaya juice. "It's so good for the equilibrium. You can go on all the scariest rides at Knott's Berry Farm and never feel dizzy. They used to give it to kamikaze pilots."

"Keep an eye on my cat, would you?" Jim asked him. "She seems okay, but you never know."

"Well, exactly. Especially with the threat of you-know-what hanging over you."

"The Death card doesn't necessarily mean that you're going to die. It could mean the death of anything. A relationship. A part of your life."

"Scary, though! *Brrr*! Watch how you drive."

By the time Jim arrived at college he was already five minutes late. Dr Friendly came out of the staff room just

47

as he was turning the corner into the main corridor and called, "James!"

"I know. Antietam. And, please, try to call me Jim."

"I just want you to know that we have some VIP visitors this afternoon. Two assistant secretaries from the Department of Education in Washington. George Corcoran from Postsecondary and Madeleine Ouster from Special."

"I see. So you want me to make sure that my class appears to be slightly less subnormal than usual."

"I'm not – I'm not *denigrating* them, James. It's just that you wouldn't train a pig to run the Kentucky Derby, would you?"

"No, and you wouldn't eat a racehorse sandwich, either. So what's your point?"

Dr Friendly inhaled, ready to say something, but then he decided against it.

Jim reached his classroom and dropped his books on to his desk. Everybody vaguely shuffled themselves into a tidier sort of slouch, and Washington took off his baseball cap. Jim paced around for a while, looking at them. Maybe, in the final analysis, Dr Friendly was right. Maybe he was wasting his time and the taxpayers' money. But he had only to look at their expectant faces, one after another, to know that he couldn't abandon them. He couldn't leave them with no knowledge of literature at all. That would be like keeping a child locked in its room all its life, and never telling it that there were trees outside, and other people, and sky, no matter what color it was.

"Today, I feel reasonable," he announced. "I have slept properly, showered, shaved and eaten a bowl of Chex with Greek yogurt on it. I am therefore ready to read your impressions of what I looked like yesterday."

He passed up and down the aisles between the desks, collecting their sheets of paper. "I think you guys have a grudge against paper. It starts off white and rectangular and smooth. By the time you've finished with it, you've almost managed to turn it back into wood pulp.

He held up Joyce Capistrano's effort, which was full of tiny holes. "Look at this. I wanted a shining contribution to expressive literature. What did I get? A lacy cake mat.

At the very back of the class, Nestor Fawkes tried to cover his paper with his elbows. Nestor was a sallow, unsmiling boy who came from a severely dysfunctional family. His face was always blotched with crimson spots and blue bruises. His older brother was in jail for attempted murder and his father regularly beat his mother until she could hardly walk. Nestor always wore cheap, ill-fitting clothes and his sneakers were falling apart. Jim doubted that there was any hope for him. Life was never that kind. But he had to try. If an understanding of *Look Homeward, Angel* couldn't save him, then nothing could.

"Nestor, you want to give me your paper?"

Nestor tilted his head and looked up at Jim sideways. "It aint no good."

"What do you mean it aint no good? Don't you mean 'it isn't any good'?"

"That's what I said, sir. It isn't any no good."

Jim came up close to him. "Who are you?" he demanded.

Nestor blinked in bewilderment.

"Who are you?" Jim repeated.

"Nestor Fawkes, sir."

"That's right. You Nestor Fawkes. You student. Me Mr Rook. Me teacher. You write. Me mark. In other words, try your best and don't be a pessimist. You might just surprise me."

Nestor sat with his head bowed, saying nothing. Jim took hold of the edge of his paper and slowly dragged it out from under his elbows. In extremely neat block capitals, Nestor

had printed: LIKE A MAN I SAW DEAD BY THE FREEWAY HIS
EYES EMPTY BY CROWS

He laid his hand on Nestor's shoulder and gave it a
reassuring squeeze. If Laura Killmeyer could communicate
by touch, then maybe he could, too. He wanted Nestor to
know that he had written a stark and graphic description
which was all the more shocking because of what it told
the reader much more about the person who had written
it than the person it had been written about. At the age
of nineteen, who had ever seen a man lying dead by the
highway, with his eyes pecked out? And, Jesus, thought
Jim, did I really look as bad as that? I have to give up
tequila slammers.

He returned to his desk and sat down. "Okay," he said,
"I'm going to read through your estimable efforts, and in the
meantime you can open your *Twentieth-Century American
Poets* to page one-two-eight and read 'Auto Wreck' by Karl
Shapiro. Read it three times. Read the last verse four times,
or even more, until you think you understand what he's
driving at. He says about this auto wreck,

> *Who is innocent?*
> *For death in war is done by hands;*
> *Suicide has cause and stillbirth, logic;*
> *And cancer, simple as a flower, blooms*
>
> *But this invites the occult mind,*
> *Cancels our physics with a sneer,*
> *And spatters all we know of denouement*
> *Across the expedient and wicked stones.*

Ray Krueger put up his hand. "What's 'day nooming', Mr
Rook?"

"It's when French guys take their pants down," put in

Tarquin Tree. "Everybody say, 'look at dose guys, day mooning.'"

"It's day-*noom*-ing, not day-moon-ing."

"Noom, moon, what's the difference?"

"What do you mean, what's the difference? You of all people, man! You're the one who said you wanted to work for NASA. You're going to go to the interview and tell them you want to try for a noom shot?"

Jim was used to this surrealistic banter and he didn't discourage it. All of his students heard words differently, and read them differently, if they were able to read them at all. He deliberately gave them challenging texts to make their minds work, to make them ask questions, to give them confidence. He encouraged them to dismantle words like the engines they took to pieces when they went to the college auto shop, and put them back together again.

"Okay, that's enough," he told them, lifting both hands. "It's *denouement*. Use your dictionaries for words that you don't understand. Don't mumble under your breath when you read. You're remedial English students, not half-wits. And – Dottie – you don't need a ruler to count down the lines. Be brave. Set yourself afloat on a sea of words. They'll carry you along, no problem, like the Lady of Shallott. You won't drown."

"Yes, sir, Mr Rook, sir," said Dottie, flushing hot pink and stowing her Disney ruler back in her bag.

"And, Ray – *denouement* is a French word, yes. But it means the final working out of a story or a plot. The loosening, the unraveling, when everything eventually becomes clear."

"Hey, Mr Rook, you learn something every day."

Washington eased himself back in his chair and said, "My dad says you learn something every day and you forget something every day. Yesterday he forgot who was the NBA Rookie of the Year, the year I was born."

"Julius Irving, Philadelphia," said Jim. "Now shut up and turn your wandering attention to reading this poem."

Washington stared at him open-mouthed. "How do you know that? That's amazing. Julius Irving. I can't believe you said that."

"The poem, Washington?"

When Special Class II had finally settled down into their usual state of whispering, giggling, passing messages and suppressed fidgeting, Jim leaned back in his chair with his feet on the desk and read their descriptions of yesterday's hangover. 'He looked like a ghost peering in through a dirty window.' That was Dottie's, and he gave her a six for it. 'A bowl of wrinkly sago pudding with 2 prunes for Is.' That was Mandy Saintskill, a black girl from Haiti. 'Imagine a wino carrying a crumpled-up bag with a bottle of whiskey in it but the crumples make a face.' That was Laura Killmeyer's, very psychic. He gave it four.

Suzie Wintz had written: 'A wrecked angel.' He really liked that. It was accurate. It was seductive. And it was very, very flattering. It spoke of a bruised, classically handsome face. It spoke of burned feathers and high tragedy. He gave her seven and knew that he would probably regret it.

The last paper he picked up was Jack Hubbard's. Unlike all of the others, this paper was neat and uncrumpled, as if he had scarcely touched it. The writing was extremely small, and he had to hold it closer to his nose to read it. While he did so, he could see Jack Hubbard watching him with an expression that was half-expectant and half-suspicious, optimism and cynicism mixed. 'Your face was gone and there was nothing but a blizzard in its place. You were lost behind what you had done.'

He had tried this exercise before: asking his students to describe him. They always ended up revealing far more about themselves. *You were lost behind what you had done.* It didn't sound as if he were talking about himself, but then it didn't sound as if he were talking about Jim, either. He didn't even know Jim, after all.

Jim lifted his pen but to mark Jack's work but he couldn't decide how much to give it. It was poetic, and it was expressive. It reminded him of Hart Crane, who would write lines like 'adagios of islands complete the dark confessions her veins spell'. You knew what it meant but at the same time you didn't.

He beckoned Jack over to his desk. Jack unwound himself from his chair and walked over in the sulky, loosely connected way that good-looking young men do. Suzie Wintz patted her hair as he went past, and splayed out her fingernails, which were sparkly yellow today.

Jim said, "What you've written here, it's very interesting. But I get the feeling that it's not about me. Or not just me. Me and somebody else."

Jack shrugged and didn't answer.

"I like the image of the blizzard in place of a face. That's very imaginative. Coldness, whiteness, and a total lack of focus. But what have I done that I'm lost behind?"

"Partied too hard, I guess. Drank too much."

"I don't know . . . the implication seems deeper than that."

"Well, I guess it can happen to anybody who says to hell with tomorrow."

"But am I the only one you're referring to? I can't really explain why it is, but I get the feeling that you're addressing this comment to somebody else as well."

Jack thought for a moment, his eyes giving nothing away. Then he said, "Somebody told me you could see things."

"Who told you?"

"One of the girls. She said you could see ghosts and stuff. Spirits."

"Well, that's right. I had a near-death experience when I was a kid. Ever since then, I've been able to see psychic manifestations that other people can't. Not necessarily ghosts, but auras, too, and invisible marks. I think other people could see them, if only they knew how to. They're a bit like those 3-D Magic Eye pictures made up of patterns. You just have to look at them exactly the right way."

"Have you seen anything around here? Like, recently?"

Jim shook his head. "Unh-hunh. Why do you ask?"

"It's nothing. I was curious, is all."

Jim leaned back in his chair and looked up at Jack, turning his ballpen end-over-end. "Do you have something you want to tell me?"

"No, sir. Everything's fine."

"I've been a teacher for a long time, Jack. I know when somebody's got something on their mind."

"I'm fine, sir. There's really no problem."

He went back to his desk, with Suzie Wintz's eyes following him all the way. "Such a cu-u-ute ass," she mouthed across the classroom to Linda Starewsky. Linda giggled and went pink.

"Okay," said Jim, getting up from his desk. "I've marked yesterday's work and I am amazed to tell you that it's all exceptionally good. Obviously my ravaged features brought out the creative writers in all of you. I'm not too sure about your rap, Tarquin. 'Mr Rook's face . . . what a disgrace . . . looks like a bowlful of mayonnaise.' Questionable simile and even more questionable rhyme."

"Hey come on, Mr Rook. You was a paler shade of yellow. Mayonnaise, that was your exact color."

"All right, then. I'll mark you up to five. But next time, hold the mayo."

They took so long to discuss each other's descriptions of Jim with a hangover that there was no time left to get on to the Karl Shapiro poem. Jim told them to read it again overnight; and to read it out loud, too.

"When you do that, you'll discover the background noise that Shapiro was able to create through onomatopoeic words and rhythms. You can hear the ambulance bell. You can hear the crowd. You can hear the crunching of broken glass. This poem is eye-witness stuff.

"'*Its quick soft silver bell beating, beating,/ And down the dark one ruby flare/ Pulsing out red light like an artery,/ The ambulance at top speed floating down . . . We are deranged, walking among the cops/ Who sweep glass and are large and composed . . . One with a bucket douches ponds of blood/ Into the street and gutter . . .*'

"And then he catches the shock that everybody's feeling. '*We speak through sickly smiles and warn/ With the stubborn saw of common sense,/ The grim joke and the banal resolution.*'

"And then he asks the questions we all ask in situations like this. '*Who shall die? Who is innocent?*' For this – this auto wreck – '*cancels our physics with a sneer.*'"

As everybody poured out of their study groups for recess, he collided on the corner of the main corridor with Karen Goudemark. She was dressed all in black today – black jewel-neck sweater, black skirt – and her hair was severely pinned up. She had obviously finished serving ice creams in Heaven and now she was ready to greet grieving relatives at the mortuary, giving them ideas that were entirely inappropriate for a funeral.

She dropped a large maroon folder on to the floor with a loud slap and he picked it up for her.

"I'm sorry," she said. "I'm in kind of a hurry."

"Well, I'm sorry, too."

"Why are you sorry?"

"I was out of line yesterday. The way I spoke to Roger and Chuck. The way I spoke to you. I was very hungover."

"You said your cat was jealous of me. I thought that was very flattering."

"Well, I guess you're easily flattered. How was your evening?"

"Very pleasant, thank you. Very . . . what's the word?"

"Riotous? Orgiastic? I don't know, I wasn't there."

She smiled at him, and she had the widest smile and the plumpest lips and the whitest teeth he had ever seen. She was standing so close that he was breathing the perfume that had been warmed inside her cleavage. He thought that now might be a good moment to kill himself. Maybe he could stab himself up the nose with a mechanical pencil, like those Japanese students who failed their exams. After all, life could only get worse after a moment like this.

"Professional," said Karen.

"Say what?"

"The evening with Roger and Chuck. It was professional. They were sharing some of their ideas on curriculum presentation and student enablement."

"So . . . no disco dancing? No wopping and a-bopping?"

"You have an imagination, Jim. I'll give you that."

She started walking back along the corridor toward the science block. "I have to set up a presentation on natural selection," she said. "You know we're having this visit this afternoon, from the Department of Education?"

"Oh, yes. Bruce Friendly told me to make my students

look as if they had started to crawl on dry land, at the very least."

"Bruce Friendly makes my flesh creep."

"Well, mine too. But it's character-building, having a head of department like that."

"No, it's not. He's a bigot and a throwback. And besides that, he tried to grope me."

"Bruce Friendly tried to grope you?"

"Oh, he pretended he was reaching for his coat. But who reaches for their coat with a cupped hand?"

Jim cupped his hand and looked down at it. Then he looked at Karen Goudemark, straight in the face. Standing so close to her, the very word 'cup' seemed erotic, and it took a supreme effort of will for him not to lower his eyes any further. "I'm shocked," he said.

"No, you're not. But I appreciate your sympathy."

They reached the door of Biology I. Karen said, "This is me. Maybe I'll catch you later."

"Maybe we could have a drink. I'm pretty good on curriculum presentation and student enablement."

"I can get all that from Roger and Chuck," she said; and there was a challenging look in her eyes which he recognized from what seemed a very long time ago. She was flirting with him. "Why don't you show me some wopping and a-bopping?"

"Wopping and a-bopping? For sure. It's Thursday tomorrow. Maybe you'd like to come to The Slant Club and meet my friend Meryvn. And wop. And a-bop."

"That sounds fun. What do you think I should wear?"

They were still breaking off their conversation in little flirtatious pieces when Nestor came running along the corridor, his eyes wild and his spotty face bleached with panic.

"Mr Rook! Mr Rook! You gotta come quick! It's Ray!"

"What's the matter with Ray?" asked Jim, running already.

"He's stuck! He can't get free! He's screaming with the pain!"

Five

J im ran after Nestor through the swing doors and out of
the building. He saw a crowd of students gathered and
he could heard a high-pitched howling, like a run-over dog.
He ran across the grass and pushed his way through to the
steps by the side of the arts block. Ray Krueger was standing
at the top of the steps, holding onto the steel-pipe railing
with both hands. His head was thrown back and there were
tears coursing down his face. Dennis Pease was standing
close beside him, trying to comfort him, while Clarence
the janitor was tugging at his wrists. Several girls from
Jim's class were there, too – Joyce Capistrano and Laura
Killmeyer and Dottie Osias – and they were weeping with
shock and terror.

"Mr Rook!" Clarence called out. "Whatever you do, don't
go touching the handrail!"

"What's happened?" asked Jim, climbing up the concrete steps.

"It's cold, Mr Rook. That handrail's so cold, you'll get
your hand stuck to it like Ray."

"Stuck to it? What are you talking about?"

Dennis said, "He was leaning over the handrail, talking
to Laura, and all of a sudden he couldn't get his hands free.
He kept saying, it's cold, it's cold, it's burning me. And we
tried to pull his hands away but we couldn't, and I can tell

you something, Mr Rook, this mother is *cold*, and I mean cold to the max."

Jim came up to Ray and held his face in his hands. "Ray! Ray, listen to me, this is Mr Rook here. I've come to help you!"

But Ray's eyes were rolling up into the back of his head and he was quaking with pain. He looked as if he were going into shock, and it was only because his hands were stuck to the handrail so tightly that he didn't fall down.

"Come on, Ray, everything's going to be fine. Did somebody call nine-one-one? Paramedics and fire department?"

"Yes, sir," said Nestor, who was close by his elbow. "They told me six minutes."

Jim looked at the handrail that Ray was clutching so tightly. It had a frosty bloom on it, with a few sparkles that caught the sun, and it was so cold that it was actually smoking. From what he could make out, it was frozen all the way along, from the bottom of the steps to the front door of the arts block. Ray's hands were white except for his fingertips, which were blueish crimson.

Next to Ray's right hand, an empty red industrial glove gripped the railing surrealistically. "That's mine," said Clarence. "I tried to pry him free but even my glove got stuck fast."

"Ray, listen to me," said Jim, putting his arm around him. "Everything's going to be fine. The paramedics are on their way and what we're going to try to do is warm this handrail up a little to get you free." He turned to Clarence and said, "Think you can connect up a hosepipe to the college hot-water supply?"

"Yes sir, Mr Rook! There won't be no problematical difficulty with that!"

"Then do it, will you? And bring a hacksaw and a hose connector."

He turned back to Ray. Ray had stopped moaning now, but his teeth were chattering and he was letting out little gasps of pain. He was so young, too. He hadn't started to shave yet, even though his upper lip was wispy with a black mustache.

"My hands, Mr Rook," he kept whimpering, rolling his head around and around. "They're burning. They feel like they're on fire."

Jim heard the sound of sirens whooping in the distance. "Come on, Ray. Just hold on a couple of minutes. The paramedics are almost here."

"But they're burning! They're burning! My fingers are burning! My fingers are burning and I can't get them free! *Aaaaagggghhhhhhhhh!*"

Jim clutched Ray close to him. He saw the ambulance swerve into the parking-lot, and thought what an irony it was, that he had just been telling them about the ambulance in Karl Shapiro's poem – '*wings in a heavy curve, dips down,/ And brakes speed, entering the crowd*'.

At the bottom of the steps, where the handrail wasn't frozen, Clarence was attacking it with a hacksaw, while two students frantically unrolled a long black hosepipe from the college boiler-house.

Two paramedics came running across the grass and up the steps. One was Hispanic, with a smooth calm face. The other was a tall red-headed woman.

"Don't touch the handrail!" everybody shouted at them, a chorus of fright. The red-headed woman snatched her hand away and said, "What? What's happening here?"

"The handrail's frozen," Jim explained. "It must be fifty degrees below. Ray put his hands on it and now he can't get them free."

"*Frozen*?" asked the Hispanic paramedic. "Was this some kind of a practical joke?"

The woman immediately went up to Ray and inspected his hands. The ends of his fingers had now turned black, and his knuckles were a deathly blueish white.

"Severe frostbite," she said. "Both hands are already necrotized right up to the wrists. And it's advancing fast."

"Necrotized? You mean his hands are actually *dead*?"

The other paramedic was calling into West Grove Memorial Hospital, telling them what to expect. "Severe frostbite. Yes, you heard that right. *Frostbite*." When he was finished he nodded toward Clarence and the other students. Clarence had already sawn through the handrail, and now he was coupling up the hose.

"This your idea?" he asked Jim. "Good thinking. You don't want to warm his hands up too quick."

Ray was shuddering and bleating and his eyes had rolled right back up into his head, so that only the whites were showing. The woman gave him a shot of ketamine to deaden the pain. Then she said to Jim, in a matter-of-fact tone, "I used to work in Chicago. I've seen this kind of thing before, people getting frozen to their car-door handles or their front doorknobs. I was walking on Michigan Avenue once and I went blind because my eyeballs had frozen. If somebody hadn't pulled me into a shop doorway I could have lost my sight."

"So what are you telling me?"

"I'm telling you that if the hot-water trick doesn't get him free, we're going to have to cut him free. The frostbite is spreading to his wrists already, look. I don't know how this could happen, but we have to act fast."

"Jesus. But his *hands*—"

"I'm sorry. We don't have any alternatives."

Jim shouted, "Clarence! Is that hot water running yet?"

"Yes, sir, Mr Rook! It's flowing right now, maximum full top blast."

The woman paramedic examined Ray's eyes, and took his pulse and his blood pressure and his respiratory rate.

"His body temperature's way below normal. His blood pressure's dropping and he's going into shock."

"Look," said Jim. The blueish whiteness had spread up Ray's wrists to his forearms now, and his hands were black, as if he were wearing gloves.

"Where's the goddamned fire department?" asked the Hispanic paramedic, impatiently.

"Can't you just saw this section of the handrail off?" Nestor suggested. "Just this section that he's holding on to."

The woman shook her head. "At this kind of temperature, the hacksaw will probably freeze to the rail. But we could try it."

"Clarence!" called Jim. "Fetch that saw up here, will you?"

But at that moment, with a loud rubbery bang, the hose connector burst away from the handrail, and the hose lashed from side to side like a cornered snake, spurting scalding-hot water in all directions. Several students were caught by the spray, and there were screams of pain and hysteria.

"Pipe's busted free, Mr Rook!" shouted Clarence. "It's all blocked up inside of that handrail, blocked up with solid ice. Going to take something more than hot water to clear that out! Look!"

Jim looked down, and saw thick, brownish slush dripping from the severed handrail, the consistency of marrowbone. The cold inside the handrail was so intense that the hot water from the hose had started to freeze, almost as soon as Clarence had connected it up.

Ray suddenly sagged. The woman paramedic said, "Keep him upright! I don't want him to tear his hands off!" Jim shifted around so that he could hold him under his arms and heft him up higher. The woman paramedic said, "He's gone into arrest!" and the man opened up his first-aid box and picked out a hypodermic. With complete calmness, he filled it with adrenalin and passed it over to the woman. She lifted Ray's sweatshirt and jabbed the needle directly between his skinny ribs, into his heart. He convulsed, and threw his head back, but his pulse started again, and he let out a thick, cackling breath, and then another.

The woman paramedic checked his arms. The dead whiteness had reached almost up to his elbows, and the grayish black tinge of death was relentlessly following it, like Indian ink staining a blotter. She said, "I'm sorry about this. I don't have any choice. The speed this frostbite is spreading, we have to get him free right now, right this minute."

The other paramedic turned to Jim. His face was smooth and his eyes were as placid as stones. "You have to look at it this way, sir. If his hands were trapped in a fire, you'd have to make the same decision. I can't imagine how this handrail got so cold, but we have to release this boy or else we'll be going to his funeral."

Jim nodded. "Okay. Go ahead. Just don't let him suffer too much."

"He won't suffer, sir. The ketamine's kicked in. And Rachel's the best there is."

The woman paramedic said, "Find me a table. Quick as you can. Something to rest his elbows on. How about you, sir? Do you think you can manage to keep on holding him up?"

Jim said, "Sure. Washington – can you help me?"

"No problem," said Washington, and bent down so that Jim could seat Ray on top of his back.

Nestor came out, dragging a small wooden table behind him. The Hispanic paramedic took it, and slid it under Ray's elbows to support them. At the same time, the woman paramedic was collecting out of her bag everything that she would need for an amputation. Jim saw the sun glint on her saw, and he had to turn away. He found himself looking at a grinning skull badge sewn onto the sleeve of Ray's sweatshirt. God, he thought. How appropriate.

Deftly, the woman paramedic laid out all of her instruments – saw, scalpels and needles, as well as swabs and pads. As she was doing so, the first firetruck arrived, honking and wailing, and a crew of firefighters came waddling across the lawn, carrying axes and breathing equipment. But by now there was nothing they could do. The Hispanic paramedic had already strapped a transparent plastic mask over over Ray's face, to give him oxygen and anesthetic, and the woman was tightening tourniquets round each of Ray's arms, just above the elbow.

"Do you have to amputate them so high up?" asked Jim. "At least if he had his elbows—"

The woman paramedic said, "He's deep-frozen right up to the middle of his forearm. Unless we amputate right up here, there's a strong chance that we'll leave some necrotic flesh, which will mean that he's very susceptible to later infection. Gangrene, which could kill him."

She looked at Jim sharply. She had green eyes and ginger freckles across her nose and there was a determination about her which Jim found both daunting and reassuring. If she had the courage to cut off Ray's arms above the elbows, to save him from dying, then he guessed that he had the courage to help her.

"All of this external tissue is dead," she said, prodding the black scabby skin that covered Ray's fingers and forearms. "In most cases of frostbite, the dead tissue is not much more than a shell, and when it peels off, which it eventually will, you'll have nothing but pink babyskin. Excruciatingly sensitive, of course. But at least it grows back."

"But this skin isn't going to grow back?"

"Not in my opinion, no. What's spreading in his body here is total frostbite. All of the muscles, bone and tendon are frozen solid. Here, look."

She picked up a scalpel and cut a deep slit in Ray's wrist. She opened it wide with her fingers, and even Jim's inexperienced eye could see that his flesh was white and solid, like deep-frozen pork, and that his veins were filled with crystals of crunchy maroon blood.

"At the rate this frosbite is developing, it's going to reach his shoulders in fifteen minutes."

The West Hollywood fire chief came up – a short, bristly man with a walrus moustache.

"Hi, Rachel. *Cómo le va?*"

"*Muy bien, gracias. Y usted?*"

"*Muy bien.* What the hell's happening here?"

"Major surgery, I'm afraid. Can you just ask your people to clear all of the students out of here? This is going to be something that they won't want to see."

"You want us to cut that handrail free? We're carrying hydraulic cutters. Won't take us a minute."

"Sorry, chief. It won't make any difference. And every second counts."

Jim was fascinated by the way in which she could talk and work at the same time. She picked up her scalpel and started to cut into Ray's left arm, just above the elbow. The tourniquet was so tight, and his arm was so frozen, that he hardly bled at all – just one big red droplet which rolled down on to his elbow and dropped onto the table underneath.

"*Madre mia,*" said the fire chief. "I think I've seen it all now."

"Please," Rachel asked him; and it was almost a command. "Please tell all of the students to go back to whatever it was that they were doing before. We don't need a crowd of hysterical spectators, not now."

The fire chief saluted. "Yessir ma'am," and went back down the steps.

Rachel continued to cut into Ray's arm. Dennis turned his head away, but Jim watched in horrified fascination, even though he couldn't stand the soft, slicing sound of it. Rachel dissected a large square of skin and fibrous tissue from the underlying muscles. The flesh was scarlet, like raw chuck steak. She picked up her shining saw and started to cut through Ray's humerus bone, just above the place where it flared out to meet the elbow. Jim closed his eyes but he could still hear the sharp, *kvetch-kvetch-kvetch* of the sawblade, cutting through human bone. When he opened them again, he saw that Ray's arm was completely detached, leaving his frozen left hand still gripping the handrail.

He swallowed hard, but his mouth filled up with bile and half-digested Chex. Almost all of the students had been cleared away by the firefighters, but he saw a figure underneath the shadow of the large cypress tree in back of the main college building. He strained his eyes, and he could see that it was Jack Hubbard, in his black jeans and black shirt, his eyes invisible behind his sunglasses, watching. A firefighter called out to him to leave the area, but he ignored him and remained where he was.

But Jim didn't have time to worry about Jack Hubbard. His back was aching from holding up Ray's unconscious weight, while Rachel was bent over in concentration, doing some incredibly fiddly needlework.

Ray shivered, but Jim knew that he was deeply unconscious. Washington shook his head and said, "Oh, man. I don't know whether I can take this. Oh, man."

"Please, Washington. Hold on a little longer."

"I'm trying to, man. But, man."

Rachel said, "In the old days, when they didn't have anesthetic, they used to use the circular method for amputation. You cut off the skin, muscles and bone at successively higher levels, so that the skin met afterwards over the other tissues. It was quick, that was the best thing about it, but it didn't always give you a satisfactory stump. The method I'm using here takes a little longer, but it gives you a much better stump."

"A much better stump? Oh, sure." Jim began to feel faint, and to see tiny prickles of light in front of his eyes. "The flap method, huh?"

"That's right. See here, I'm going to ligature all of the severed blood vessels in his arm. Then I'm going to take this flap of flesh and stitch its sides and its end."

Rachel was so matter-of-fact that it was difficult to grasp the enormity of what she was doing. She was saving Ray's life. But he would never be able to feel anything with his fingers any more: never be able to stroke another animal, and feel its fur. Never be able to touch a woman, and feel her softness through his fingertips.

Jim could see only bone; and gristle; and a complicated array of veins and arteries.

Rachel sewed up his left arm. She must have been good at needlecraft at school, because she managed to tug the flap back together. The surgical thread made a soft rasping sound as she pulled it through his skin.

When she came to amputate Ray's right arm, Rachel found that the frostbite had already advanced beyond his elbow. His forearm was black and crusty, his upper arm was already white, and she had to cut his arm off just below the shoulder. Again, that slicing sound. Again that rasping saw. Then, over an hour since Nestor had first come running up the corridor to tell Jim what had happened, Ray was laid on to a gurney, his two stumps sticking up like the

68

handles of a wheelbarrow, and carried, tilting, down to the ambulance.

> *Stretchers are laid out, the mangled lifted*
> *And stowed into the little hospital.*
> *Then the bell, breaking the hush, tolls once,*
> *And the ambulance with its terrible cargo*
> *Rocking, slightly rocking, moves away,*
> *As the doors, as an afterthought, are closed.*

Jim leaned back against the brick wall, feeling as if he had been in a fight, every muscle aching. Washington eased himself up and stretched his back and said, "Man . . . I don't believe it. I just don't believe it. Nestor stood with his hands covering his face, as if he could only bear to look at the world through the cracks in his fingers. Ray's amputated arms, along with Clarence's glove, remained where they were, frozen, all clutching the handrail.

The fire chief came up and looked at them uneasily, uncertain what to do. But it was already becoming obvious that the frost was melting. The ice crystals on the handrail faded away – and with an abruptness that startled them all, Clarence's red industrial glove dropped on to the concrete. In less than a minute, Ray's left arm dropped off, too, followed by his right.

Jim said to Dennis and Washington, "It's okay now. Why don't you two take the rest of the day off? I think you've both done more than enough, and thank you."

Washington swallowed and nodded. "I just want to know how this could have happened. And *why*, man? Ray was the harmlessest guy in the world."

Jim gave him a slap on the back. "Being harmless never guarantees that you won't be harmed. Sometimes the opposite. Now, go on. We'll talk this out later."

As Dennis and Washington went down the steps, Lieutenant Harris came stamping up them, closely followed by Dr Sigmund Fade, from the coroner's department. Lieutenant Harris was short and stocky, with scrubby ginger hair. He wore a white short-sleeved shirt that was almost transparent with sweat. Dr Fade was tall and pale, with a large complicated nose and hands that fluttered weakly around in the air like butterflies.

"I've seen some stomach-churners, believe me," said Lieutenant Harris, jerking his head toward Ray's blackened arms. "But this – well, *phwooph*. What do you think could have caused that handrail to freeze like that?"

"No idea," said Jim. "I guess there must be some kind of scientific explanation, but I'm damned if I know what it is."

Dr Fade noisily rolled plastic gloves on to his hands. Then he hunkered down and picked up the severed arms one after the other. "No doubt that it's frostbite," he said. "You remember that guy who was shut all night in the meat-chiller at Coolway Packers? Was he black? He came out looking like Al Jolson."

"But that was in a meat-chiller and this is right in the middle of the open air on the hottest day of the week."

"You should have your forensic people check the inside of the handrail. There might be traces of gasses in it, like liquid nitrogen, maybe. Or even liquid hydrogen."

"It still beats me how anybody managed to freeze it like that. And why? Didn't have any enemies, did he, this Ray Krueger? Anybody who might have wanted to turn him into a human icicle?"

"He's one of the best-liked students in the class," said Jim. "He's kind of uncontroled, sometimes. It's a psychological thing: he comes bursting out with all kinds of wacky remarks. But otherwise . . . no, he doesn't have any enemies. Not so far as I know. And it strikes me that freezing a handrail is a pretty unreliable way of getting your own back on somebody you don't like. Just about anybody could have touched it."

"How about generally?" asked Lieutenant Harris, mopping the back of his neck with his handkerchief. "Any disaffected students been making threats to the college lately?"

Jim shook his head. "We've been pretty much free of that kind of thing, thank God. We keep a weather-eye on the nerds and the geeks and the loners and we keep a watch for student cults, too."

"What do you mean, like neo-Nazis?"

"Anything. We've had some neo-Nazis and some neo-Black Panthers and some neo-Shining Path. We've even had some neo-Zapatistas. But so far we've usually managed to coax them back into the mainstream of student life. You know what kids are like at this age. Arrogant and shy. Desperate for respect. You only disaffect them if you ignore them."

Lieutenant Harris cautiously ran his fingertips along the handrail. "Somebody would have to know science to do this, right?"

"I don't know. But it's probably worth checking all the college laboratories to see if there's any liquid gas missing. And it's probably worth talking to Dr Kelley, he's the head of physics."

They both fell silent for a moment while they watched Dr Fade carefully lifting the two severed arms and sliding them into a black plastic bag. A TV news cameraman was standing right behind them, recording every moment in close-up.

"Don't you have anything better to do, you ghoul?" Lieutenant Harris asked him.

"Just doing my job, lieutenant. Same as you."

Lieutenant Harris turned back to Jim. "I don't know," he said, shaking his head. "Every time I get called out here, and it's something to do with you, it's always weird. It always seems to get cleared up, and I never know how. I think it's you, Mr Rook. I think you attract weirdness, like a magnet."

"Who's to say what's weird and what isn't?" said Jim. He was tempted to mention the mensroom incident, too, but his instinct advised him not to say anything. He thought that Lieutenant Harris probably had enough to worry about, as it was.

Jim said, "I'd like to be the one who tells Ray's parents what's happened, if I can. I know them pretty well."

"Sure thing. I appreciate it. Not a job that I was especially relishing. I'll catch you later."

Six

Jim walked down the steps and along the diagonal path that led back to the main college building. As he did so he saw that Jack Hubbard was still standing under the tree. As he came nearer, however, Jack came out into the sunlight and cut across the grass.

"Mr Rook?"

"How's things, Jack?"

"I think I need to talk to you, Mr Rook."

"Can't it wait until later? Right now I have to go tell Mr and Mrs Krueger that their only son just lost both of his hands."

"This concerns Ray. Leastways, I think it does."

Jim continued to walk toward the college entrance and Jack fell in beside him. "Something happened to my dad in Alaska. I don't exactly know what it was, but it's been worrying him. Ever since he came back from his expedition, he's been so jumpy. It's like he's been waiting for something bad to happen."

"Oh, yes?"

"Something's happened to me, too. I keep having nightmares, almost every night. I'm caught in a blizzard and there's something following me. I can't see it, but I know it's there. It's right behind the snow, and it wants to kill me."

Jim stopped, one eye scrunched up against the sun.

"This is all pretty disturbing. But what does it have to do with Ray?"

"Maybe nothing. But maybe everything."

"Go on, tell me."

Jack took off his sunglasses and wiped the perspiration from his forehead with the back of his hand. Now that Jim could see his eyes, he looked far less sinister than he had when he was standing under the cypress tree. In fact he looked vulnerable and frightened.

"As soon as we moved into the house on Pico, Dad hung up these Inuit fetishes in every window and every doorway. They're all different, but they all have a seal-skull, and fishbones, and bear's teeth, and a piece of fur from an Arctic wolf. They're supposed to keep out evil spirits.

"Every night before he goes to bed he says this ritual kind of chant. I don't think he knows that I've heard him doing it. I know a few words of Inuit but I don't know what this chant means. And it was my mother who was Inuit, not him. So why is he doing all this chanting?"

He hesitated for a moment, and then he said, "My father gave me this." Out from the neck of his shirt he produced a flat piece of ivory, in a lozenge shape. It had been drilled at one end so that Jack could wear it on a leather thong. Jim lifted it up and peered at it closely. It had been carved on one side with the scrimshaw picture of a figure standing alone – a figure with no face. On the other side there were four vertical marks.

"What is it?" asked Jim. He was deeply disturbed the four vertical marks, which looked just like the marks that had been drawn on the mirrors in the frozen washroom. And he was even more disturbed by the appearance of the figure, which vaguely resembled the hooded figure on his Tarot card.

"It's an Inuit talisman. The fur-trappers always wear them,

to protect them against bad luck. He said I had to wear it always, just in case."

"Just in case of what?"

"That's what I don't really know. But Dad's always talking these days about blizzards and snow and things that people can't see. Every evening I go home and he's sitting in front of the television watching his video about his journey across the glacier to Dead Man's Mansion. Sometimes he's kneeling right in front of the television screen, about three inches away from it, staring into it. It's spooky. But all you can see in the picture is snow, and these two dark shapes, the other two guys who went with him.

"And whenever I ask him what he's looking for, he says 'nobody'. But he keeps on looking."

They entered the college building and walked along the corridor. It was unusually hushed, and from one of the open classrooms Jim could hear the sound of a girl sobbing. He expected that Dr Ehrlichman, the principal, would probably close the college for the remainder of the day. "Come into the classroom," he said. "I have to get my stuff. Then I really must go see Ray's parents."

Jack followed him back to Special Class II. "I told my Dad about the washroom being frozen. He said, 'You're pulling my chain, aren't you?' and tried to make a joke about it, but I could tell that he was worried about something. But I showed him that it was true because I still had my sweatshirt in the trunk of the car – you know, the one that was frozen, and it was still hadn't thawed out properly. One of the sleeves was all ice."

"Go on," said Jim, as they left the classroom and walked toward the college parking-lot. The hot sun hit them as they opened the doors.

"He acted real strange. He took the sweatshirt and threw it in the trash and said that I should never wear it again.

He'd buy me a brand new one. I argued about it, because I really liked that sweatshirt, but he wouldn't listen. In the end he got so angry I gave it up.

They reached Jim's car. Jim threw his case into the back seat and opened the door with a deep *crronk* sound.

"So what's the connection with Ray?" he asked.

"Ray really dug that sweatshirt because it had a badge sewn onto the sleeve from Dad's expedition. Maybe you saw it: Dead Man's Mansion Two Thousand – and a picture of a laughing skull with a fur-trapper's hat on. So the next morning I took it out of the trash when my Dad wasn't looking and I brought it to college and I gave it to Ray. I thought – you know – shame to waste it."

"So when Ray was stuck to the railings, he was wearing your sweatshirt? The same sweatshirt that was hanging in the washroom when it was covered with ice?"

Jack nodded. "I was thinking about it and thinking about it, and even though it sounded crazy, I knew I just had to tell you."

Jim was silent for a long moment, thinking. Then he said, "I think I'd better take you up on that invitation to visit your Dad. Listen – let me deal with Ray's parents first. Then I'll give him a call. And listen – I've heard crazier things, and I really appreciate your telling me."

He climbed into his car, started it up, and backed out of his parking space. Jack stood and watched him go, and even when Jim reached the college gates and swerved out into the road, he was still standing there, as if he were afraid to move, because the rest of his life was coming to get him.

Jim walked up the path of the Krueger home on Burnside Avenue and pressed the doorchimes. He looked around while he was waiting. The Kruegers lived in a single-story house with grayish green walls, its roof overhung with flowering bougainevillea. Seashells had been embedded in the concrete around the porch, and there was a handmade ceramic plaque of four smiling faces which was obviously supposed to be the Krueger family. Jim pressed the doorchimes again. It was so hot out here that he had to lick the sweat from his lips.

Eventually a thin, pale-faced woman came to the door, wiping her hands on her apron. She looked washed out and tired, and her hair was straggled by the heat. Jim knew that Ray Krueger's father had suffered a crush injury at work when he was loading palettes, and that his mother had to support the whole family on his redundancy money and whatever she could earn as an office cleaner. Ray had wanted to go out to work, too, to help her: but she had been adamant that he should improve his reading and writing.

"Why, Mr Rook!" she said. "What a surprise! And just look at me, all hot and bothered!"

"Hallo, Mrs Krueger. Is your husband home, too?"

"He's always at home, since his accident. Why don't you come on in?"

Jim stepped into the small hallway, crowded with photographs of the Krueger family; and then through the door into the living-room, where Mr Krueger was sitting in front of the television with a rug over his knees. He was a bull-headed man, with a thick neck and a deep torso, but Jim could tell that all of the strength had gone out of him. His cropped hair was prematurely white and there were dark circles of suffering under his eyes.

"Mr Rook, what brings you here?" he said, picking up the TV remote and switching off the baseball. "Ray aint been in no trouble again, has he?"

"He's been doing his homework religiously," said Mrs Krueger. "He sits down at seven and he doesn't move from the table till he's finished it."

"He is improving, aint he?" asked Mr Krueger. "You haven't come here to tell us that he's going to flunk English?"

Jim's mouth was dry. "It's nothing like that. I've come here to tell you that there's been a serious accident at college. Ray's lost both of his arms."

Both of the Kruegers stared at Jim as if he had spoken something in a foreign language. Slowly, Mrs Krueger raised one hand to her mouth, and her eyes began to fill up with tears, but Mr Krueger still seemed totally perplexed.

"You're saying what? You're saying Ray's lost what?"

"I'm desperately sorry, Mr Krueger. Ray's arms were trapped. The paramedics had to amputate to get him free. Otherwise he would have died."

"Trapped? Trapped, like how do you mean, trapped?"

As simply as he could, Jim explained what had happened. But how can you explain frostbite on a hot day in June? How can you explain flesh that dies in front of your eyes? He could see that neither of the Kruegers really understood what he was talking about.

"He's very seriously hurt. But right now, he needs your optimism, more than your tears. He could still be a vet. When he's recovered, he could still do almost anything. He's been through a terrible experience, Mr Krueger, and he's going to suffer shock and emotional trauma but he's going to need us all to give him hope."

"Hope?" said Mr Krueger. He clutched the arm of his chair and slowly managed to heave himself on to his feet. His pelvis had been shattered and he could only walk with a rolling, laborious sway, like Captain Ahab on the deck of the *Pequod*. "He's the dumb kid of a couple of dumb parents, and he never had a chance, right from the moment that he was born. Now he's lost his arms and you're talking about *hope*?"

He staggered over to the sampler that hung over the fireplace, *Blessed Be We*. He lifted his right fist and Jim knew what he was going to do; and Mrs Krueger probably knew, too. He smashed the glass, and the broken picture-frame dropped into the hearth.

Mr Krueger stamped on it, until it was completely shattered. Then he looked up at Jim and said, "There aint no hope, Mr Rook. All of those things that I was going to do. All of those things that I was going to be. I never had the brain for it. And then what happened, when I found the stupidest job on earth, just to make a honest living? I got crippled. But I always thought that Ray was going to do better. Ray was going to lift himself out of this life. Ray was going to make good where I never could. But God dumps on people like us, generation after generation. There aint no hope, Mr Rook. And the worst thing is, pretending that there is. That's what kills people. Not the hope. But pretending that there is."

There was a long silence. They stood amongst the shattered glass. Mrs Krueger stood with her face covered with her hands.

"I'll give you a ride to the hospital," said Jim.

It was well after seven p.m. before he returned home. As he inserted his key into the lock, Mervyn's door opened and Mervyn appeared, wrapped in a cerise kimono, his hair pinned up with tortoiseshell barrettes.

"I saw the news," he said, grasping Jim's hand, and squeezing it tight. "Wasn't that terrible, that poor boy? And they said you were so brave, holding him all the time."

"Thanks, Mervyn. It's been kind of a long day."

"I looked in on Tibbles Two a couple of times. She looked bored, so I sang her a couple of torch songs. To tell you the truth, she wasn't very impressed."

"Apart from that, though . . . ?"

"Apart from that she's wonderful. And so are you. You don't know what it's like, living next to a hero."

"The feeling's mutual, Mervyn. Thanks for everything."

Jim opened his front door and walked into his apartment. He whistled and called out, "Tibbles! Tibbles Two!" but there was no sign of her anywhere. He walked into the kitchen and opened the freezer. He had a choice of beef lasagne or vegetable lasagne or *ojingu chim,* Korean stuffed cuttlefish, which he had bought in a moment of madness at the local Korean deli. He decided against all of them, and shut the freezer again.

He didn't really feel hungry. He was too distressed after what had happened to Ray this afternoon. All the same he knew that he needed something to eat, so he took a sliced loaf out of the breadbox and made himself a folded-over sandwich with eight slices of Oscar Mayer's baloney and two whole kosher pickles which dripped vinegar all the way down his wrist.

He walked back into the living-room, and as he did so, he saw a picture on his new widescreen TV of Dr Ehrlichman, his college principal. Dr Ehrlichman was saying, "Everybody worked together, you know, and everybody co-operated. It was a terrible thing to happen to a young student, but everybody rallied around, as they always do whenever something goes wrong at West Grove."

"Which is unusually often, isn't it, Dr Ehrlichman?" asked the TV reporter. "In the past five years we've had several fatalities, a considerable number of injuries, and dozens of unexplained phenomena. Would it be right to say that West Grove Community College is *haunted*?"

Dr Ehrlichman snapped, "I'm in the education business, mister. Not the California Psychic Society."

Jim sat down in his favorite creaky basketwork armchair and flicked through the channels until he found *Captains*

Courageous in black and white, with Spencer Tracy and Freddie Bartholomew.

As he was chewing his sandwich and watching television, he thought he saw a shape out of the corner of his eye. He slowly turned his head; and as he did so, his chewing slowed down too. Gradually, he stopped masticating altogether, and his mouth stayed open, displaying a pulpy lump of wet white bread marbled with pale-brown baloney.

Tibbles Two was standing on her hind legs on the back of the couch. Upright, not moving, not swaying, perfectly balanced. She was staring at him with both eyes wide open, her ears flattened back against her skull. In her mouth she was holding a single Tarot card.

"TT?" said Jim, and swallowed the rest of the sandwich so hard that he almost choked. He stood up and walked across to her, but she remained where she was, still upright, unwavering, her eyes still staring at him. "TT . . . do I get the feeling that you're trying to tell me something?"

He took the Tarot card out from between her teeth. It was the same card that he had picked last night, the hooded figure standing alone in the snow. It was still nameless. He turned it this way and that, and then he said, "You're trying to tell me something, right? This is a privileged communication from the spirit world, right?"

Tibbles Two said nothing, of course, but yawned, one of those wide supercilious yawns that cats always give you when they think that you're being slow on the uptake.

"You're putting me back on track, aren't you? You're telling me to follow the clues that really matter."

Tibbles Two jumped down from the back of the couch and padded into the kitchen in search of milk. Jim stayed where he was for a while, turning the Tarot card over and over between his first and second fingers. *The blizzard covers your face. You are hidden behind what you have done.*

At last he went to his briefcase and opened it up, and took out his college directory. He flicked it to the pages marked Students' Parents, and ran his finger down until it reached 'Hubbard, Henry'. There was a regular number and a cellphone number. He dialed the cellphone first, guessing that Jack's father would probably be at the studio, working on his documentary. It rang for a long time before it was eventually picked up.

"Henry Hubbard speaking."

"Mr Hubbard? This is Jim Rook, Jack's English teacher from college."

"Oh, yes?"

"I'm sorry to disturb you, but we've had a serious incident on campus today. A young student was seriously hurt."

"That's too bad. Jack wasn't involved, was he?"

"No, sir. Not directly."

"What do you mean 'not directly'? What happened?"

"A student lost both of his arms. Ray Krueger, I don't know if Jack's ever mentioned him. Poor kid was only nineteen."

"That's terrible. That's really terrible. But if you'll forgive me for asking, why are you calling me?"

"Because he lost his arms to severe frostbite."

"*Frostbite?*"

"Worst case the paramedics had seen since a man was trapped in a deep-freeze. Except that this wasn't in a deep-freeze. This was right outside, in the sunshine, in an ambient temperature of eighty-four degrees."

There was a lengthy silence. Then Henry Hubbard said, "I still don't see how this concerns me."

"Jack told you about the washroom freezing over, so he tells me. I was just wondering if maybe we could meet and – you know – discuss it. Seeing as how you're the only expert on cold weather conditions that I can think of."

"I'm sure there must be somebody at UCLA who's much more qualified to help you."

"Well, maybe there is. But I'd like to talk to you about Jack, too, how he's settling down in class."

"He's not adjusting?"

"That's something we ought to talk about face to face."

Another lengthy silence. Then, "Okay . . . why don't you come by the house around nine tonight? That's not too late, is it?"

"That'll be fine. And watch the TV news, if you get the time. You'll see what happened to young Ray."

"I'll try my best, Mr Rook. I'll talk to you later."

Jim hung up and turned around to Tibbles Two. "Are you satisfied now?" he demanded. But Tibbles Two simply tucked his front paws into his furry chest and closed his eyes. Jim went over and picked up the Tarot card that the cat had brought him. The figure was still standing in the snow, still waiting. The stars were still shining in the black sky above its head.

He went to his bookshelf and took down one of his battered Morocco-bound encyclopedias, the ones that his father had given him when he graduated. He looked up astronomy and found pages and pages of star maps, constellations and clusters, to see if he could find any configuration of stars which matched the pattern on the card. Maybe it had some significance, maybe it didn't, but most background details in the Tarot had some symbolic meaning, whether they were distant castles or lobsters swimming in rivers or figures with their faces turned away.

The afternoon sun slowly swiveled around the apartment as he turned the pages of the encyclopedia sideways and diagonally and upside-down. The pattern of stars on the card was so distinctive that he couldn't believe it wasn't a real constellation. Yet he couldn't match it anywhere. And every now and then he would find himself stopping his search to think about Ray, his hands burning with cold, going through agonies that it was almost impossible for anybody else to imagine.

He gave up looking for star patterns. He went to the fridge and stared into it, to see if there was anything else that he wanted to eat. He closed the door again and went back into the living-room. Tibbles Two had opened her eyes now and was staring at him fixedly.

"Who sent you?" asked Jim, sitting down beside her. "I don't believe you came here by accident, no way."

Tibbles Two jumped off the couch and up on to the chair where Jim had been sitting while he was looking through the star constellations. She hesitated for a second, and then she jumped up on to the table. Her paw caught the encyclopedia, which was resting on the very edge, and it toppled over.

"Hey!" said Jim, and lunged forward to catch it. But it didn't fall instantly. He had never seen anything fall like this before. It dropped to the floor in slow-motion, as if the afternoon air were as thick as treacle, and as it fell its pages flicked over, page after page, almost as if somebody were thumbing through it.

It fell only an inch beyond his outstretched fingers. It was like something out of a dream. It hit the floor and bounced on its spine, and then it slowly settled on to the carpet, with its pages wide open. Tibbles Two had already jumped off the table by now, and made her way to the other side of the room, where she turned and watched Jim with that same supercilious look in her eyes.

Jim picked the book from the floor. It had fallen open at a page about the signs of the Zodiac, and the movement of stars and planets. On the right hand side of the page was an illustration of the northern sky on the night of 16 June 1816. With one or two minor exceptions, the pattern of the stars was identical to the stars depicted in the Tarot card.

The caption read: *The star-pattern which presaged the 'year without a summer'*.

Jim said, "What is this? Some kind of joke?"

Tibbles Two gave a low, soft mewl. Jim glanced at her but didn't say anything. He was beginning to think that she wasn't a cat at all, but a human spirit which had been reincarnated as a cat.

"You should give me a clue, you know that?" he told her. "You should tell me who you are. Then I can give you some of the things you liked when you were a person. A drop of bourbon in your milk, maybe? Or low-cal cat food? You should tell me. After all, you can bring me Tarot cards, and you can open encyclopedias to the relevant page. What's to stop you from telling me your name?"

But Tibbles Two remained inscrutable, and started to descend into a deep, larynx-rattling sleep.

Jim laid the encyclopedia back on the table, took his glasses out of his shirt pocket, and started to read. In early June, 1816, astronomers had noticed a highly unusual configuration of stars in the Northern hemisphere. It was a configuration that had first been mentioned in Old Norse writings in the year 505, although the same pattern had been discovered painted on the walls of caves in the Belgian Ardennes, and these had probably dated from several hundred years BC. The Norse name for the configuration, in the old twenty-four-rune alphabet, was The Harbinger of Cold. Its appearance was said to be a warning that the world was going to be punished for some unspecified sin.

The morning after the stars' appearance, at eight a.m., snow started to fall on most of the north-east and parts of northern Pennsylvania. The Danville *North Star* in Vermont

85

reported snowdrifts up to twenty feet, and spring crops all across the United States were devastated.

The freeze was even worse in Europe, where blizzards crossed Britain and France, crops failed, and thousands died. One strange by-product of the icy summer of 1816 was that the poet Percy Bysshe Shelley and his wife Mary were forced to stay indoors in their villa near Lake Geneva, where Mary whiled away the time by writing *Frankenstein*. And Frankenstein's monster, in the end, leaps on to an ice-raft in the Arctic Ocean, and disappears into the darkness.

The next time the same pattern of stars appeared was on the night of 14 April 1912, when it was sighted over the North Atlantic Ocean by Robert Philips, the first officer on board the *Mesaba*. He drew a rough picture of it in his diary, which would have been forgotten for ever, if 14 April hadn't seen one of the greatest disasters in modern history, the sinking of the White Star liner *Titanic*.

The encyclopedia's entry concluded, 'Although there is insufficient scientific evidence to prove it, the appearance of this particular pattern of stars always seems to presage freakishly cold weather conditions; and widescale death.'

Seven

Jim drove down to Pico Boulevard shortly after nine fifteen. The evening was still uncomfortably hot, and his room-width windshield was splattered with insects. There were rumbles of thunder far off to the south, and lightning danced across the horizon like stiltwalkers.

Pico Villas was a shabby 1960s building with a concrete courtyard and a concrete flying saucer planted with dried-up yuccas. Jim pushed open the door to the stuffy, stale-smelling lobby and found the button marked "Hubbard". He pushed it and waited for an answer.

Eventually, he heard Henry Hubbard's voice say, suspiciously, "Yes?"

"Jim Rook, Mr Hubbard. Sorry if I'm a little late."

"That's all right. Come on up. Third floor, second on the right."

Jim stepped into the elevator. It was so cramped that he was glad that he was alone. It was lined with wood-patterned Formica, too, which made it feel like a vertical coffin. It seemed to take hours to groan its way up to three; and even when it did, it remained motionless, with its doors still closed, for almost fifteen seconds. Then, with a convulsive shudder, it opened.

Henry Hubbard was waiting for Jim with his apartment door open. He was a tall, rangy man, with bristling white hair and a face that looked as if it had been eroded by years of icy-cold winds. His eyes were pale green, and his nose was large and pitted. He was very clean-shaven, as if he had just come out of the bathroom, and he smelled of Hugo Boss aftershave. He wore a green checkered shirt and pale-blue jeans, with a wide leather belt.

"Mr Rook? Henry Hubbard. Glad you managed to find us." He gave Jim a strong, dry handshake.

"Jack home yet?" asked Jim.

"He shouldn't be long. He's meeting some of his friends from college. I believe they're forming some sort of support group. They're getting themselves together to talk out their emotions about what happened to young Ray Krueger today, and Jack seemed to be very keen to be part of it. I guess it's a good way of helping them to deal with it. You know. Young kids, a trauma like that. They need to express what they feel."

"Did you see the news?"

"Yes. But, to tell you the truth, I almost wish that I hadn't. I've witnessed enough tragedy in my time, caused by the cold. I don't need reminding what frostbite can do."

Henry Hubbard led Jim through to a plain, sparsely furnished living-room. It had a distinctly rented look about it. An olive-green carpet, cheap laminated furniture. A large oil painting of an orange sun that looked like an advertisement for Minute Maid orange juice. In one corner, however, stood a huge new widescreen Sony television and stacks of videotapes, all neatly labeled; and above it was a bookshelf crowded with books on meteorology and geography and Arctic and Antarctic exploration.

"You'll have to excuse the confusion," said Henry Hubbard. "I never seem to get the chance to—"

"Hey, don't worry about it. My place is just the same. That's the trouble with living alone. That cup of coffee you left on the table in the morning, it's still there when you come home at night. I haven't trained my cat to wash dishes yet."

"Get you a drink?"

"Anything. Club soda, Coke, whatever you've got."

"Beer? Unless you're on duty or something."

"Beer's fine. I don't have any problem with beer."

Henry Hubbard brought two cans of Pabst and they sat on the leatherette couch together.

"West Grove must be in some kind of turmoil today, after what happened."

"Turmoil?" said Jim. "Turmoil's an understatement. You can't blame people for panicking. But I'm determined to find out how that railing got so cold. I'm not letting Ray sacrifice his hands and never know why."

Henry Hubbard nodded, but he kept his eyes lowered, and didn't look up at Jim once.

Jim said, "Jack told you about the washroom freezing up?"

"That's right. You still haven't found out how that happened?"

"No, but I'm working on the assumption that the washroom incident and the railing incident are directly connected."

"I wish you luck. But don't be surprised if you never find out how they happened. The cold can be like that. Full of secrets, you know? The cold . . . well, let me tell you, the cold is a different country."

They sat and drank in silence for a while. Then Henry Hubbard said, "Jack's doing okay? He seems to like his English class."

"Jack? Jack's doing fine, from what I've seen of him so far. He seems to be intelligent, perceptive, articulate. I don't think he's going to have to stay for very long in Special Class II. He just needs to find his place in the educational system, that's all. Once he's up to speed, I don't see any problems whatsoever."

"He's happy? He's not disturbed?"

"Why should he be disturbed?"

"I don't know, losing his mother. Moving around so much."

"He seems okay to me."

"That's good," said Henry Hubbard, nodding. Then, "What happened today . . . this frostbite thing. I don't really see how I can help you."

"I wanted to pick your brains is all."

"Listen . . . just because I went to Alaska, just because two of my friends got frozen to death, that doesn't mean I know anything and everything about cold weather conditions. As a matter of fact, my friends and I were exposed to minus seventy-one degrees . . . and when you consider that the lowest temperature ever recorded in the US was minus eighty – that was at Prospect Creek, Alaska, in 1971 – well, what we went through, that was pretty close to the limit. It was a miracle I got out of there alive."

"Jack seems to think that you've got something on your mind. Something to do with what happened up there."

"You said he wasn't disturbed."

"There's a difference between being disturbed and being bewildered."

"Bewildered? What about?"

"He says he's tried to talk to you about your last expedition but you always close up. He says you spend hours staring at the video recordings, looking for something, and he doesn't know what. He says you've hung up all of these Inuit fetishes, around the house; and you make him wear a whalebone talisman around his neck. From where I'm standing, I'd say that it bewilders him. He's looking for answers."

Henry Hubbard shrugged and said, "It was a tough deal, that last expedition. Very, very tough."

"So why don't you share it with him? He seems to have the feeling that he's being excluded."

"Excluded? That expedition . . . everybody in the whole world was excluded, except us. You can't share an experience like that. You can't even talk about an experience like that. I'm only making this TV program because I'm contracted to do it and I need the money. My friends are dead. If I had any choice in the matter, I'd never think about it again."

"So what are you looking for, when you stare at those videos?"

"White, that's what I see. White, white, white. I have nightmares about it. What am I supposed to say to Jack? He looks up to me, like I'm some kind of role model. But he wasn't there. He didn't see what I saw. He doesn't understand."

"He doesn't understand what?"

"He doesn't understand what it's like when you're right in the middle of that total white-out and you're sure that you're going to die."

"But you didn't die."

Henry Hubbard gave Jim a strange, defensive look, as if he had been caught taking money out of somebody's wallet. "I didn't, no. I survived. But I was closer to dying than I ever want to be again. If you want to know the truth, Mr Rook, that expedition took everything out of me. My sense of adventure, my courage, everything. It even took my pride."

Jim sat back and said nothing for a while. Henry Hubbard was clearly agitated. He kept rubbing his hand backwards and forwards across his mouth, as if he were trying to wipe away the taste of a foul-tasting kiss.

"So you feel guilty?" asked Jim.

"Of course I feel guilty. Sometimes I wish I hadn't come back . . . just died on the glacier like my friends did. What do they call it? Survivor syndrome. You don't know how many times I wish I were dead. But it didn't work out that way."

Jim said, "Why don't you tell Jack about it? I mean, not glossed over, not like a TV documentary, but the way it really happened."

"I can't. He wouldn't know what I was talking about."

"Why don't you give him a chance?"

Henry Hubbard shook his head. "He doesn't want to hear how his old man lost his nerve; and his old man doesn't want to tell him, either."

"Then why don't you try telling me?"

Henry Hubbard drank some more beer. Then he stood up, and walked around the couch. "Did you ever hear of Dead Man's Mansion?"

"Unh-hunh. Can't say that I did."

"It's a story that dates back to 1913 or thereabouts. There's supposed to be a house in northern Alaska, up in the mountains near the Yukon border, much grander than any of the cabins you usually find in those parts. They say it was built by one of the survivors of the *Titanic* disaster, nobody knows why. Guy called Edward Grace. He was supposed to have lived there all alone for years.

"I still don't know how much of the story is true. But Edward Grace was supposed to have lived there until he didn't have the strength to cut himself wood any longer, and he froze to death. They say that he's still sitting at his living-room table, mummified, along with his cat."

"His *cat*?"

"I always thought it was one of those tall tales that people tell you in Alaska. But one night in Fairbanks I got talking to an old man in the hotel bar. He was out in the wilderness once, so he told me, making seismic tests for oil, and he and his companions had gotten lost in the middle of a blizzard. He swore that – just for a moment – he had actually seen Dead Man's Mansion, although the weather had closed in so bad that he hadn't been able to get close to it. I thought he was nothing but a rambling old drunk, but when I talked to the barman, he told me that he used to be a world-famous petro-geologist. I looked him up on the Internet, and the barman was right. Senior exploration geologist for Amoco. So that's when I started to take the story of Dead Man's Mansion a little more seriously.

"I persuaded NBC to finance most of the trip, and the rest of the sponsorship came from the University of Alaska in Anchorage. I chose two volunteers to go with me – Randy Brett and Charles Tuchman. Randy was the best historian in the north-west, and Charles was a highly-qualified cartographer, and both of them were experienced climbers and Arctic explorers, too.

"We flew up as far as Old Crow, on the Yukon side of the border, and then we trekked our way westward, using two 1920s maps that Charles had found in an antique bookshop in Seattle. We also had a whole notebook full of hearsay stories about Dead Man's Mansion – where it was located, how it had been constructed, all of the legends and myths that surrounded it. One old cannery worker said that his father had not only found Dead Man's Mansion, but been inside it, too, and seen Mr Grace sitting at his drawing-room table. Apparently Mr Grace had a deck of cards laid out in front of him, from the HMS *Titanic*. This old cannery worker's father had even taken one of the cards to prove it – or so he said. He said that he'd lost it, when he moved down south.

Henry Hubbard switched on his television. "We took two

snowmobiles and we made pretty rapid progress. We were convinced that we knew approximately where Dead Man's Mansion had been built, and that if we made a systematic search it wouldn't take us more than a week to find it. But then the snow started, and the winds got up, and by day three we were struggling to make more than six or seven miles a day."

Jim turned around on the couch and looked at the TV screen. At first it looked as if there was thick white interference, but then he realized that what he was looking at was snow.

Henry Hubbard said, "It was April, and sure, you can still get plenty of snow in April, up in those latitudes, and up at those elevations. But this was worse than anything I've ever seen. The snowmobiles seized up, so we had to walk, and even though we had satellite direction-finding equipment and transponders and you name it, we were lost and we were blind and we seriously began to think that we were in a life-threatening situation."

He pointed to a dark shadowy shape on the right of the screen. "That's me . . . that's Randy, walking next to me – you can hardly see him, can you? And Charles was taking the pictures."

All that Jim could see was whirling white flakes and occasional dark flickers which might have been anything.

"Jack says you stare at the screen, real close. What are you actually looking for?"

Even now, Henry Hubbard had his eyes fixed, unblinking, on the television. "I'm looking for the fourth man," he said.

"The fourth man? What fourth man?"

"Huh! It sounds as if I'm losing my marbles, doesn't it? But after two days of crossing the mountains, we all began to think that we were four in our party, not three. We were conscious that somebody was walking with us, and after a while the feeling grew so strong that we talked about him as if he were really there."

He paused and said, "He always walked on our left."

"Did you see him?"

Henry Hubbard didn't answer, but continued to stare at the mesmerizing snowflakes. "It was a joke at first. We called him George. If anything went wrong, we could always blame George. But by the end of the fourth day it was more than a joke. We even saved rations for him.

"I didn't know about this until I got back to Anchorage, but other explorers have experienced the 'extra man' phenomenon. It goes right back to Marco Polo when he rode across the Lop Nor desert on his way to China. At night he heard spirits talking who appeared to be his companions."

He picked up a loose-leaf folder from the top of the television. "And look at this: when Sir Ernest Shackleton's ship *Endurance* was crushed in Antarctic ice in 1916, he and two others left the crew on Elephant Island and traveled eight hundred miles in a small boat to South Georgia. They landed on the deserted side of the island and climbed ranges that had never been climbed before to get help from a whaling station.

"Here, this is what Shackleton wrote: 'I know that during that long march of thirty-six hours it often seemed to me that we were four, not three. And Worseley and Crean had the same idea.' Seven years after the event, Worseley wrote that 'even now I find myself counting our party – Shackleton, Crean and I and – who was the other? Of course there were only three, but it is strange that in mentally reviewing the crossing we should always think of a fourth, and then correct ourselves.'

"And listen to this: 'Steve Martin and David Mitchell and another Antarctic veteran, Keith Burgess, came across the fourth man when they were crossing Greenland. They called him Fletch. When they came to record their journey, they put it down as a four-man crossing, and F. Letch was the fourth member.'

"The extra man has appeared again and again – whenever it's cold, whenever people are lost. Frank Smythe climbed up Everest in 1933 and always felt that he had a companion, somebody to catch his rope and save him if he slipped. He kept food for his companion, too. And here – in February 1957, a fellwalker called Dennis Goy was caught in a blizzard in Britain's Lake District. He came across some recent footprints in the snow and followed them. But the footprints stopped, right in the middle of a vast expanse of untouched snow."

"Don't you think that you can put it down to physical and mental stress, in very remote locations?"

"Probably."

"You're not sure, though, are you? You're not sure at all?"

"Well, he seemed so damned real at the time. George, or Fletch, or whatever you care to call him. When I came back, I talked to my father-in-law about it. He's a full-blooded Inuit, and he lives in Inuvik now – he's an archivist for Inuit culture. He said that he's plenty of stories about the 'extra man'. He has friends who were saved from the wilderness, just like me; and all of them talk about somebody who came to guide them out of the snow. The Inuit won't talk about him much. But my father-in-law said that they call him an Inuit name meaning 'snowman'."

"Did the snowman save *you*?" asked Jim.

"Me? No, those are only stories."

"But you've done all of this research . . . and you're still looking for him," said Jim, nodding toward the television.

"Maybe just to satisfy myself once and for all that he

didn't exist. I survived and my two companions died. I don't like to think that it was down to anything other than luck."

Jim could sense that Henry Hubbard had more to tell him, but he fell silent, as if he couldn't bring himself to put it into words. He was obviously still grief-stricken by the deaths of his fellow-explorers; and it must have been hell to put together a documentary of everything they had done together. Jim could see dozens of photographs spread out across the living-room table, photographs of smiling bearded men in bright Arctic clothing, their arms around each other, laughing, optimistic. Now there was nothing left but the snow flying across the television screen.

"I'm going to ask you a straight question," said Jim. "Can you think of any possible connection between your expedition to Dead Man's Mansion, and what's been happening at West Grove College?"

Henry Hubbard gave him an almost imperceptible shake of his head.

Jim waited, and then he said, "You don't think that, somehow, that there's a connection between the cold you experienced in Alaska, and the the cold we're experiencing here? And that Jack could be the link between them?"

"How could there be? It's not logical."

"Ray Krueger losing his hands to frostbite, that wasn't logical either. I'll tell you something, Mr Hubbard. A whole lot of terrible things happen in this world that aren't logical, but they happen nonetheless. No summer in the year 1816. The *Titanic* going down. Frost in June. Blizzards in mid-July."

Henry Hubbard said nothing more. Jim finished his beer and said, "Well, I'll be going then." He stood by the door for a moment, watching Henry Hubbard in front of his snowstorm television, and then he went out and closed it behind him.

As he climbed back into his car, he hesitated. The evening was still warm, but he distinctly felt a faint chilly draft blowing on the back of his neck. He looked around him, at the car-cluttered concrete driveway in front of Pico Villas, but he couldn't see anybody. He looked behind, to Pico Boulevard, with its noisy, jostling traffic. Nothing unusual.

But then he thought he heard a tapping noise off to his right, coming along the cracked concrete sidewalk. A slurring tap, as if somebody were sweeping a stick from side to side, and giving a little sharp tap at the end of every sweep.

He looked around, but he couldn't see anybody at all. This wasn't a part of town where people walked very much. Yet the tapping noise continued, and it sounded as if it were coming closer. *Tap!* – sweep – *tap!* – sweep – *tap!* – until it sounded so near that Jim involuntarily took a step back.

Then he saw them. On the sidewalk in front of him, glittering marks appearing, one after the other, like footprints. They came nearer and nearer, and for one moment he thought that they were heading directly toward him. He pressed himself back against the side of his car, and the footprints passed in front of him, only a few inches away. At the same time he felt a sub-zero coldness unlike any coldness that he had ever felt before. This wasn't the bracing snap you felt on the ski-slopes; or the fresh cold you felt when you were out on the ocean. This was a dead, still cold – a cold that could crack rocks, or freeze a body for ever. This was the cold of the Arctic night, in which penitent monsters floated through the darkness on rafts of pallid ice.

A prickling sensation crept all the way up Jim's back. One hand was resting on the top of his car door, and he felt the metal being emptied of all of its evening warmth. The windshield suddenly bloomed with white frosty flowers.

His breath smoked. Over by the sign that said Pico Villas, a yucca plant sparkled with ice. Whatever it was that was passing him by, it was capable of lowering the temperature within a fifty-feet radius all around it. Its footsteps continued until they reached the signboard and then they stopped, although the tapping continued, *tap – tap – tappity – tap*, nervous, inquisitive and quick.

Jim didn't dare to move, didn't say a word. If there were any kind of spirit here, he would normally be able to see it. But he couldn't make out anything except frosty footsteps, and even these were rapidly beginning to fade. Cautiously he knelt down and touched one, and it was made up of thousands of needles of sparkling ice, infinitely fragile.

The tapping continued. Patient, but threatening. There was no doubt in Jim's mind that whatever this invisible presence actually was, it had come looking for Jack. He strained his eyes but he couldn't see even the vaguest ripple in the evening air. Maybe he was losing his ability to see spirits and phantoms and out-of-body travelers. Or maybe there was something very different about this particular manifestation. Maybe the intense cold was capable of creating a creature that couldn't be seen and couldn't be touched, while it could freeze everything around it with complete impunity.

It waited for a while, and Jim had the impression that it was trying to sense whether Jack was any place near. It didn't seem to be interested in him at all, in spite of the fact that he was less than twenty feet away, his thin arms covered with goosebumps.

After more than five minutes, the tapping started up again, and then the sweeping, and the frozen footsteps continued eastward toward Rexford Drive, sparkling in the streetlight, until they finally disappeared. Jim waited for a moment, listening. Then he swung himself into his car and found his keys with fingers that were numb with cold. He started up the engine and pulled out of Pico Villas in a cloud of smoking rubber.

He was sure of it now: a malevolent spirit was searching for Jack. It had tried to locate him at school, without success, and Ray Krueger had been frozen instead. Now it had arrived at Jack's home. Even if it was somehow connected with Henry Hubbard's ill-fated expedition to find Dead Man's Mansion, it obviously wasn't looking for Henry Hubbard himself. So what did it want? And why? What could Jack have possibly done to make it so determined to freeze him?

As he drove home, Jim kept thinking about that tapping sound along the sidewalk. It reminded him of something, but he couldn't think what. But when he stopped for a red light at the intersection of Venice and Palm, he saw a specialist pet store on the opposite side of the street called Strictly For The Birds. In the window, in a huge domed cage, sat a large red and green parrot, the kind of parrot that Long John Silver might have carried on his shoulder.

Long John Silver, from *Treasure Island*. And who was the terrifying character in the opening chapters of *Treasure Island* who had tapped his way down the road to the Admiral Benbow Inn? Blind Pew.

That was the *tap*-slur-*tap* that he had heard. The tapping of a blind man's stick, feeling his way. A blind man, or a sightless spirit. Why else would it have frozen the washroom, unless it had been obliged to rely on its sense of touch or smell to tell it that Jack was there? Except that he hadn't been there, of course – only his sweatshirt. And why else would it have frozen Ray Krueger, unless it had believed – mistakenly – that it was freezing Jack?

The lights changed to green and the car behind him blasted

its horn. Jim gave the driver a wave of apology and took a left turn toward home.

There was one thing more that worried him: if the spirit had come to Jack's apartment block, looking for him, then it knew that it had frozen the wrong person. That meant that Jack was still in danger, and so were any other students at West Grove Community College who happened to get in its way.

Eight

The next morning, Dr Ehrlichman held a special non-denominational prayer assembly so that the students of West Grove Community College could all pray for Ray Krueger's recovery in their own way.

Dottie Osias gave an address which she had written herself, and which Jim found deeply touching. She delivered it in a high, asthmatic voice, her cheeks flushed with determination.

"Ray Krueger is one of those people who seem to believe that the universe is something they've invented in their own minds, and that everybody they meet is somebody they've invented, too. I guess in a way you could say that he thinks he's God. But just like God, he always takes special care of the world that he's invented. He's a leading member of the West Grove environmental study group. He went upstate last summer to fight for the redwood forests, and he spent three days helping to rescue a stranded minke whale on Will Rogers State Beach.

"Everybody knows how tender Ray can be with animals; but not everybody knows how tender he can be with people, too. He suffers from an emotional problem which sometimes makes him shout out rude and aggressive things he doesn't really mean. That upsets quite a lot of people, and I can understand that. But behind all of those outbursts, there's a very special person who cares so much for everybody he meets; and I mean everybody.

"I remember my very first day at West Grove. I didn't have any friends because my family had just moved to Los Angeles from Cleveland, Ohio. I was overweight. I was asthmatic, and all of the eucalyptus trees in the college grounds didn't help that any. Nobody spoke to me and I didn't even know where I was supposed to go for class. I was too embarrassed to ask anybody, because I was in Special Class II, which meant that I was the next best thing to a retard.

"I was sitting alone crying. But Ray Krueger saw me, and came over to me, and asked me what was wrong. It took me a long time to tell him, but he was so patient and understanding; and in the end, when he found out that I was going to the same class that he was, Mr Rook's class, he put his arm around me and led me there, and told me that I was going to have a great time in Special Class II. It wasn't a class for retards, he said. It was a class for people who cared.

"Well, Ray Krueger cared. And we care for him. And no matter which God we say our prayers to before we go to sleep at night, let's make sure that we make a special plea for Ray, to help him through his pain, and to bring him back to us. Not intact in body, maybe. But intact inside of his head. Because the world needs people like Ray. I know that I sure do."

As everybody filed out of assembly, Jim was immediately approached by Dr Friendly, accompanied by a toothy fortyish woman with bouffant ginger hair and a bright green suit.

"James . . . I want you to meet Ms Madeleine Ouster, from the Department of Education. She was supposed to make a visit yesterday, but obviously, under the circumstances . . ."

With a jingle of gold bangles, Madeleine Ouster shot out her hand. "Mr Book! I've heard so much about you and your Special Class II."

"Not Book, Rook," Jim corrected her.

Madeleine Ouster blinked at him. "Book, Rook?"

"Maybe you'd be good enough to take Ms Ouster along to your first class, James," said Dr Friendly. "You know . . . show her why West Grove Community College thinks that you're such a star."

Jim gave him a look that would have killed a parrot on the opposite side of the street. But he laid his hand around Madeleine Ouster's shoulders and guided her toward Special Class II, while he gave her his full 'gravely disadvantaged but bravely struggling' speech about his remedial students. "These young people are having to fight against impossible odds, just to be literate. Everything's against them. Society, their parents, television, peer-pressure. You have to understand how courageous they are."

"What interests me, Mr Book-Rook, is your approach. Most remedial teachers rely on simple texts like Dr Seuss and children's classics. But you're teaching your students Walt Whitman and Hart Crane and Marianne Moore."

"They may find it difficult to read and write but that doesn't mean that they're stupid," Jim told her. "I think it's a mistake to start them on overly simple texts, especially at this age. They get bored too quickly, and who can blame them? You're nineteen years old and you're going to read about *Green Eggs & Ham* for two weeks? The answer is to challenge their intelligence, to make them think. Once they've started to think, their syntactic skills soon catch up."

He pushed his way into the classroom. As usual, it was

chaos, with Mandy Saintskill and Christopher L'Ouverture rapping together, and the air thick with flying pellets. Washington Freeman III standing on his head and Suzie Wintz was flapping her hands to dry her freshly polished nails. Instantly, however, the pellets stopped flying and everybody was sitting at their desks with earnest, attentive looks on their faces. Jim made a point of looking to see if Jack Hubbard, and there he was, thank God. Obviously the blind spirit hadn't returned to Pico Villas last night.

Jim said, "I want to introduce you to Ms Madeleine Ouster, from the Department of Education in Washington. Ms Ouster is interested in the work we've been doing here in Special Class II. I hope you'll welcome her and show her that this remedial class is the equal of any other English class in the country."

Tarquin Tree stood up and gave Madeleine Ouster an exaggerated bow. Then he clapped his hands and said, "Everybody here . . . says aloha and hi . . . and looks you in the eye . . . like a piece of the sky . . . we're going to show you . . . that we know the lingo . . . much better than bingo . . . so you go back . . . and say we're on track . . . and you're going to be . . . Ouster the Booster!"

Everybody applauded, including Jim. Madeleine Ouster gave a thin smile and said to Jim, "Why don't you carry on? I'll sit in the corner and watch. This promises to be educational, to say the least."

Jim walked up and down the aisles between the desks, saying nothing at first. He waited for quiet. He waited for everybody in the class to guess what he was thinking about.

Eventually, he said, "We stood and prayed for Ray today. Ray would want us to carry on with our work, bettering ourselves, day by day, the way that he was trying so hard to better himself. So that's what we're going to do. But we're not going to forget that we have a classmate and a friend who needs our love and our support, and that what happened to him could have happened to any one of us.

"We're going to start our study today with 'The Ball Poem' by John Berryman; and I want you to think about this poem in context with what happened to Ray yesterday, and in context with your own lives, and all of those things that you take for granted.

> *What is that boy now, who has lost his ball,*
> *What, what is he to do? I saw it go*
> *Merrily bouncing, down the street, and then*
> *Merrily over – there it is in the water!*
> *No use to say 'O there are other balls':*
> *An ultimate shaking grief fixes the boy*
> *As he stands rigid, trembling, staring down*
> *All his young days into the harbor where*
> *His ball went.*

He finished the poem and then he asked the class to discuss it. What did it mean? How did it apply to their own lives, their own growing up? Joyce Capistrano said it was a cynical poem that said life is tough and nobody is ever going to help you. Washington said, "It means you gotta stand on your own two feet, even when you think you lost everything, the same way Ray lost his hands. You gotta say, I lost that ball for ever, man, and I aint never gonna see that ball no more, and all I can do right now is forget it, and go on, because there aint no point in crying over lost balls or wasted days."

Nestor Fawkes put up his hand and said, "I had a ball once. It was red and yellow. I saved up my allowance for it. I took it home and my father stuck his whittling knife into it. He said that would teach me."

"And did it teach you anything, do you think?" asked Jim.

"It teach him his old man's the meanest piece of shit in greater Los Angeles," put in Tarquin.

But without looking up, Nestor said, "It teached me not to hope for nothing."

"It taught you not to hope for anything," Jim corrected him.

"That, too," Nestor agreed.

"Okay. But was that a good lesson or a bad lesson?"

"I don't know," Nestor shrugged. "But if don't never hope for nothing you don't never get disappointed, do you?"

They talked a lot about Ray. They were all burning to talk about him, and Jim encouraged them. He wanted them all to put their feelings into words – even if those words were mixed up and ungrammatical or downright obscure. "Ray – shoot – I feel like I lost a crown off of my head," said Tarquin.

Eventually he approached Jack. He stood very close, but Jack kept his eyes fixed on the floor. "Jack, what do you feel?" he asked him.

"I hardly knew him," said Jack.

"But you must feel something, surely?"

"I feel . . . I feel like the sins of the father are visited on the child."

"I don't get it. You're not trying to suggest that Ray's father had anything to do with this?"

"There are other fathers. There are other children."

Jim knew what Jack was trying to tell him. He said, very softly, "Okay . . . maybe we can talk about that later."

"He's so mo-oo-ody," said Susan Wintz, fluttering her eyelashes.

At the end of the class, Jim set them the task of writing a short poem or essay about Ray – "but remember 'The Ball

Poem' and don't make it slushy. I don't want it to sound like something out of a movie, all misty-eyed and sentimental. The movies are not life. This is life."

When the classroom was empty, Madeleine Ouster came up to him and said, "Well."

Jim was leafing through Walt Whitman's *Specimen Days in America*, looking for a classroom text. She stood there and said nothing else, and after a little while he looked up at her.

"Just 'well'?" he said. "This is where I usually get the speech on how I mustn't divert from the approved curriculum; and how on earth can rappers and homeboys and fat dumb kids who can hardly read a Donald Duck comic be expected to appreciate John Frederick Nims."

Without hesitation, Madeleine Ouster said,

> *Who gather here will never move the stars,*
> *Give law to nations, track the atom down.*
> *For lack of love or vitamins or cash*
> *All the red robins of their year have gone.*

Jim took off his glasses. "John Frederick Nims, 'Penny Arcade'. I'm impressed."

"And I'm impressed, too, Mr Rook. What I saw in this classroom today has no equal in any English remedial class that I've seen anywhere. I'm going to ask Dr Ehrlichman if he'll consider releasing you for a period of time so that you can come to Washington, DC and join my new consultative action force on American literacy."

"And are you going to ask me if I want to go?"

"You're a teacher with a great sense of personal duty, Mr Rook. I can see that for myself. My action force has the urgent task of reversing the diminishing literacy levels all over the country. It's absolutely vital for our survival as an educated nation. We need skills like yours, Mr Rook, and we need them very badly."

"How long would this be for?"

"It depends on what results we achieve. A year minimum."

"That would mean leaving this class."

"I'm sure West Grove College has access to other English remedial teachers."

"Yes, but – this is my class. What do you think that somebody like Nestor Fawkes is going to do without me? How do you think Tarquin Tree is going to express himself to a teacher who only believes in Janet and John?"

"It's precisely that kind of dedication that I need, Mr Rook."

"I don't know . . . it's very difficult."

Madeleine Ouster opened her pocketbook and took out a card with the crest of the Department of Education on it. "Why don't you think it over and call me? But let me just say this: if you become a member of my literacy action force, your next step can only be up. You'll have access to all of the special educational units in the country. You'll be able to try your ideas not just in one classroom, on twenty young people; but in hundreds of classrooms all across America, on thousands of young people. I appreciate your loyalty to your students here. But why should they be the sole beneficiaries of this wonderful gift that you have to offer?"

Jim said, "You haven't talked about money."

"Because I'm not trying to bribe you, that's why. I'm just trying to make you see what good you could do – not only for yourself, and your personal career, but for young people everywhere." She paused, and then she said, "If you're interested, though, the pay will be roughly twice what you're making here."

Jim tapped her card against his thumbnail. For the first time in a very long time, he was lost for words.

Madeleine said, "We've already had our initial remit meetings, and I'd like you to join us as soon as you possibly can. Sleep on it, why don't you, and call me before eleven tomorrow at the Westwood Marquis?"

She shot out her hand again, and firmly shook it, and then she was gone. Jim looked down at the open book on his desk. *'With me, when depress'd by some specially sad event, or tearing problem, I wait till I go out under the stars for the last voiceless satisfaction.'*

At that moment, Jack Hubbard came in, and stood by the door.

"Hi, Jack."

"You saw my old man last night."

"That's right. He told me all about his expedition to Dead Man's Mansion. Pretty harrowing stuff."

"He was kind of upset. He said that you were trying to make out that there was some kind of connection between what he did in Alaska and what's been going down here."

"That's because I'm pretty sure that there is. And I think my suspicions were confirmed last night when I was just about to leave your apartment block." He told Jack about the tapping, and the coldness, and the footprints made of ice.

"Tapping?" said Jack, frowning. "I've heard tapping, too. I guess it started about a week after we arrived here. I never knew what it was."

"It's some kind of presence, Jack, I'm sure of it. For some reason I can't see it, the way that I can usually see spirits and ghosts and stuff. But the tapping makes me think that it's blind, and if spirits can't see you then maybe you can't see them either."

"What do you think it wants?"

Jim closed his book. "I don't want to frighten you, but

110

I think that your hunch about the sweatshirt was right. It's looking for you . . . but because it's blind it can only hunt you down with its sense of smell."

"Why do you think it's looking for me? I didn't have anything to do with Dead Man's Mansion."

"I think your dad knows. I'm afraid he gave me the impression last night that he wasn't being totally honest with me. Not lying, exactly. But being very economical with the truth."

"I've asked him so many times, but he just won't answer."

"The answer lies in that blizzard, Jack. Something happened up in Alaska – something bad. Whatever it was, that presence is looking to freeze you solid."

It was another sweltering afternoon and the smog was even more lurid than ever. During afternoon recess, Jim prowled around the college grounds, looking for any sign of the blind, invisible spirit that was searching for Jack. He had a strong sense that it was close, but there was nothing to betray its presence. No icy footprints, no sudden drops in temperature, no sparkling frost.

He was crossing the lawn behind the science block when he saw a bright flash of light. It flashed again, like a heliograph. Shielding his eyes with his hand, he walked over to a group of girls who were sitting together under the wide, shady branches of the cypress tree.

"Trying to attract my attention?" he asked. "Or trying to dazzle me?"

Laura Killmeyer smiled and said, "Sorry, sir," and put down the large circular mirror that she was holding. "I was showing Joyce her grandfather."

"You were what?"

"I was showing Joyce her grandfather. It's a magic thing. You do this special ritual and then you look in the mirror and the person you want to see is standing right behind you."

"You're kidding me, aren't you?"

"Oh, no," said Joyce. "I actually saw him. Only for a second, but it was definitely him."

"I saw my cousin," put in Linda Starewsky. "She was wearing the same red dress she was wearing the day she died."

"You mean you can see dead people in the mirror?" asked Jim. "Spirits and things like that?"

"That's right. It's called spirit-shining. My aunt showed me how to do it. She can see ghosts and all kinds of different spirits. She saw a Red Indian wonder-worker once, standing in her hallway. She can use a mirror to tell how long people are going to live, too, but she doesn't like to do it any more. When you look in the mirror you can see the person running round and round the room, and the number of times they run around is the number of years that they're going to live. She did it with a friend's son. He ran round the room twenty-two times and then he disappeared."

"So what's this ritual?"

"You slice an apple in two and eat half facing east and the other half facing west. Then you kiss the mirror and say, *'Mirror, mirror, take this kiss; and show me all those ones I miss.'* You cover your eyes with your hands, and then you look in the mirror through your fingers."

"And that's when you see the spirit?"

"That's right. But only in the mirror. If you turn around, there's nobody there, and that spirit will never appear to you again."

"I didn't realize you took this witchcraft thing so seriously."

"It's really interesting, and it works. And I only ever do good witchcraft, like curing people's colds and getting rid of warts and stopping people from having nightmares. I can do this amazing spell which stops your nose from bleeding, like instantly! But I don't have anything to do with Satan."

"You believe in Satan?"

"I don't know, and I don't really want to find out. A friend of mine had a beautiful new dress once, and I tried to work this spell so that the dress would vanish from her closet and reappear in mine. But when I started to do it, I smelled an awful burning smell and I saw two red eyes looking at me through the net curtains, and so I stopped. Maybe it wasn't anything, but it really scared me."

"Do you think I could do it?" asked Jim.

"What, have somebody's dress appear in your closet?"

"No, the spirit-shining."

"You don't need to, do you? I thought you could see spirits anyhow."

Jim shook his head. "Not all of them, as it turns out. I don't think I can see blind spirits, for example."

"Well, you could see them in the mirror. Joyce's grandfather was blind, wasn't he, Joyce?"

Joyce nodded. "He had cataracts when he was really old. He used to ask me to sit on his lap and describe things to him. What the clouds were like, what color the flowers were. He used to call me his Little Pair of Eyes."

Jim checked his watch. It was time for his next class. He left the girls under the tree and started to walk back toward the Liberal Arts building. As he opened the door to enter it, he was sure that he felt a chilly draft on the back of his neck, and his skin prickled. He turned around but there was nobody there, not even any frosty footsteps on the concrete pathway. He went inside, and the corridors were noisy with jostling students. But he still couldn't rid himself of the feeling that the icy presence was even closer than ever.

*   *   *

That evening he drove over to West Hollywood and picked up Karen Goudemark from her mother's orange-painted house on North Kings Road. Karen was wearing a red hairband and a low-cut white T-shirt and a pair of tight red pants. She was all bounce and brightness and dimples and fresh-washed hair.

Jim had changed into his best blue and yellow Hawaiian shirt but he hadn't had time to press his chinos. He was also acutely aware that the recent hot weather had caused the sole of his left shoe to start coming unglued.

"You look terrific," he told Karen, as she climbed into the car. The passenger door closed with an excruciating *grronk*. "You know who you remind me of? Olivia Newton-John in *Grease*. *'You're the one that I want, oo-oo-ooh*!'" He popped his fingers and did a John Travolta dance around the back of the car. The sole of his shoe bent underneath his foot and he lost his balance and fell against Karen's mother's mailbox, knocking it sideways at forty-five degrees.

He straightened the mailbox to a reasonably acceptable tilt and then climbed into the car. Karen looked at him with her hand pressed tightly over her mouth, her eyes dying to laugh. Jim started the engine and swerved away from the curb. "All right, now you know why John Travolta's famous and I'm not," he told her.

"I thought you were much better than John Travolta."

"You did? Well, maybe I was. When it comes to controlled staggering, John Travolta's an amateur."

She sat back and let the warm evening breeze blow through her hair. "Didn't you used to have a pink car?" she asked him.

"That's right. A Lincoln. I felt like Jayne Mansfield in it. But I found out after I bought it that the woman who used to own it committed suicide in the driver's seat. Carbon monoxide, from the tailpipe. When they found her,

'Kentucky Rain' was playing on the car radio. Every time that song came on, the inside of the car started to smell like exhaust, and I used to have this terrible suffocating feeling. So I sold it. I'm too sensitive to stuff like that."

"How do you cope with it? I mean, how do you deal with seeing a ghost? I'd be terrified."

"They're more frightening when you can't see them. Like this thing that's being going around the college, freezing everything."

"You really think it's some kind of ghost?"

"Ghost, spirit, entity. I don't know what you'd call it. I don't really have any idea what it is. It could be somebody who's recently died, trying to get their revenge. You'd be amazed how vindictive some dead people can be."

"You're kidding me."

"Not at all. A lot of dead people can't get it into their heads that they're not alive any more – especially people who were killed in sudden accidents. They're angry with the people who killed them, and they're angry with their friends and relatives because they're all still alive while *they're* nothing but spirits.

He stopped at the traffic signals and then he said, "Jack Hubbard's father was the only survivor of an expedition up in Alaska that went badly wrong, and I've been wondering whether this spirit that's bothering us is one of his dead companions."

Karen said, "You're serious, aren't you?"

"Of course I'm serious. This is a serious situation."

"But a *ghost*?"

Jim swerved on to the freeway, inviting a furious barrage of horn-blowing from a Mexican family with a huge yellow couch on the back of their pick-up.

"I may be wrong. It may not be a ghost. It may be a demon."

115

"Oh, of course. A demon. Why didn't I think of that?"

"Because you don't believe in demons, that's why. But anything that the human mind can imagine can exist. I've had a run-in with an apparition that was made out of nothing but human fear. That's all. Fear, and it took on shape of its own. We underestimate ourselves so much. Look at Uri Geller. He's realized that the human mind is powerful enough to stop clocks and bend spoons. But what he hasn't realized is that the human mind can create living creatures. If you're afraid of the dark, let me tell you this: the dark will take on a shape, and the dark will come to get you, and the dark will do all of the things that you're afraid it's going to.

"I was reading last year about this woman in Cincinnati who didn't like to hang her robe on the back of her chair because when she switched off the lights it looked as if there was a hunchback in her room. Her daughter accidentally left her robe over the chair one night, and in the morning the woman was found strangled with the sleeves of her robe tied tight around her neck."

"You're trying to frighten me."

"No I'm not. I'm just making you aware that there are plenty of things in this world that we don't really understand, and some of them are very dangerous."

"So what are you going to do? About this ghost, I mean. Or demon, or whatever it is."

"I have to find out what it wants – and then, I don't know. I guess I have to exorcize it, or whatever."

Jim was silent for a while. He wished the subject of ghosts hadn't come up. He was too worried about Jack Hubbard, and malevolent spirits certainly weren't the stuff of light-hearted seductive banter.

"You're going to like the Slant Club," he said, as they turned off at the Venice exit. "It's kind of a cross between

116

the Cage Aux Folles and the Viper Lounge. And the pina coladas are a work of art."

They parked outside the bright pink neon entrance, and Jim handed his keys to a car jock dressed in a satin mini-skirt and sneakers. It was still early, but the club was already crowded with pretty girls who were girls and pretty girls who weren't girls and good-looking young men in Versace coats and Emporio Armani pants. Jim was known to the heavily built dyed-blond doorman because he was a friend of Mervyn, and he and Karen were ushered right inside.

Mervyn was in blazing form that evening – probably because he knew that Jim had brought Karen here to impress her. Dressed in yellow peacock feathers and turquoise ruffles, he sang 'St Louis Woman' and 'The First Time Ever I Saw Your Face' and ended up with the earthiest version of 'Tiptoe Through The Tulips' that Jim had ever heard.

"Having fun?" he asked Karen, laying his hand on top of hers.

She smiled at him with her eyes sparkling in the pink cabaret lights. "It's different."

"I was offered a job today," he told her.

"A job? Doing what?"

"Sitting on the Department of Education's Literacy Action Force in Washington, DC. Madeleine Ouster asked me. It's good money – almost twice what they're paying me here."

"So you're going take it?"

"I don't see how I can. I can't leave Special Class Two right before their exams. Besides, I have this problem with Jack Hubbard to work out. I can't risk anybody else getting hurt."

"But surely somebody else can deal with it? The police are on to it, aren't they? It shouldn't be your responsibility in any case."

"The police don't believe in supernatural presences."

117

"Maybe they don't. But have you thought that you might be wrong, and it isn't a supernatural presence? Maybe it's a meteorological aberration, that's all. They had hailstones in Australia last month, as big as footballs."

"I saw footprints made out of ice."

"Yes and maybe they weren't footprints at all. Think about, Jim. You've admitted yourself that this is the first spirit that you haven't been able to see."

"Because it's blind, that's why."

"Why should that make any difference? Stevie Wonder isn't invisible, is he, just because he's blind?"

Jim finished his drink and twiddled with the paper parasol. "Okay, I'll grant you that."

"So think about that job, Jim. I know how well you get on with your class. It's legendary. But there are times when you have to stop thinking about other people and think about yourself. This could make all the difference to your career. You could end up with Madeleine Ouster's job one day."

"You're not trying to get rid of me, are you? This is our first date and already you're trying to pack me off to the east coast."

Karen laughed and shook her head. "Come on," she said, "why don't you take me for a drive? We can look out over the city lights and pretend we're seventeen again."

They left the Slant Club and Jim drove them up into the hills, to a favorite vantage point up in Franklin Canyon. Karen was right: it was just like being seventeen again, sitting in the car and watching the glimmering lights of Los Angeles scattered across the night.

"Do you know who I always wanted to be?" said Karen. "I wanted to be Jane, in the jungle with Tarzan, looking after the wild animals."

"You're doing the next best thing, teaching biology to the students at West Grove College."

"I wanted to wear a skimpy leopardskin bikini and swing through the trees."

"Very appealing, but regrettably I couldn't have joined you. I could never even climb the ropes in phys ed. Lack of upper-body bulk, that's what the teacher told me."

She shifted herself closer to him, and took hold of his hand. "You would have made a wonderful Tarzan. Thoughtful, loyal, caring. You're all of those things."

"No, it's the cry. I couldn't even manage the cry without coughing."

They were silent for a while. Karen leaned her head back and looked up at the sky. "I always get frightened, looking at the stars. They make me feel like my life is so insignificant."

"You're right. It is insignificant. And so is mine, and so is everybody else's. When anybody makes fun of the kids in my class, I always ask them why they think their life is so much more important than any of *their* lives. We're all ants, in the end."

"You're not very politically correct, are you? You're supposed to tell them that everybody's life means something."

"An ant's life means something. It just doesn't mean as much as the ant thinks it does."

Karen pointed to the north. "What's that star there? That bright one?"

"Don't ask me, I'm not very hot on astronomy."

"It's not the Pole Star, is it?"

Jim turned his head around and peered at the star with more concentration. It was so much brighter than the other stars clustered around it that at first he didn't realize that he was looking at a highly distinctive constellation. It was the same pattern of stars that appeared on the tarot card – the pattern of stars that was supposed to presage death by freezing.

119

"Jim – what's wrong?" asked Karen.

"It's those stars. They're a seriously bad omen."

"Oh come on, Jim, you're letting this whole thing get to you."

"I can take you to my apartment and show you a tarot card with that exact same pattern of stars on it."

"Well, I don't really think so. I think you'd better take me home."

"Karen—"

"You've can't be responsible for everything and everybody, Jim. The world will still go around without you."

Jim didn't say anything, but drove the Cadillac back on to the road, and headed back toward West Hollywood. He switched on the radio but it was playing "Kentucky Rain" and so he switched it off.

Nine

Jim slept badly that night. He imagined that he was walking through the snow in a bleak, Arctic landscape, and that a blizzard was pouring past him like a plague of white locusts. Through the snow he thought that he could make out a tall hooded figure, dressed in white, plying its way across the tundra, with its face always turned away from him.

He was cold and he was deeply frightened, but he couldn't wake himself up. He tried to walk faster, to see if he could find out what the figure was, and if it could help him, but it always kept away to his left and well ahead of him – so far that he couldn't decide if it were really there or not.

By the time the morning sun came slanting through his venetian blinds and woke him up, he felt exhausted, as if he had been trudging for miles and miles across cold and unforgiving terrain. He knew it was ridiculous, but he had to sit up and check his toes to make sure that he didn't have frostbite.

He scrubbed his hands through his hair, and vigorously scratched. It was only then that he caught sight of Tibbles Two sitting upright on the back of the wooden chair on the opposite side of the bedroom, perfectly balanced, perfectly still, staring at him. When he sat up she yawned and licked her lips.

"I don't trust you, TT," he said, heaving himself out of

bed. "I'm not even sure that you're a normal cat. What cat sits on the back of a chair like that? Haven't you ever heard of gravity?"

He went into the kitchen and put some espresso coffee on to perk. Then he opened a can of catfood and dug a spoon into it to fill TT's bowl. The only trouble was, the spoon wouldn't penetrate it. He dug at it again, and then he realized what was wrong. The catfood was frozen solid.

Frozen.

Urgently, he searched the kitchen. He opened cupboard doors and slammed shut them again. He looked into the broom-closet. Then he went into the living-room and circled around, searching for any signs of icy footprints. There was none. But then he stopped and looked at the vase of yellow orchids in the middle of the coffee-table. The water inside it was completely frozen, and the petals themselves sparkled with hoar-frost.

It had been here. The presence had been here, right inside his own apartment. It hadn't only been a nightmare, unless his nightmare had somehow taken on a life of its own, and prowled around his apartment while he was asleep.

"It was here!" he shouted at TT. "That goddamned thing was here, while I was asleep! Call yourself a watch cat? Why didn't you mew or something? Or yowl? Or miaow?"

TT ignored him and went to stand by her empty food-bowl, flattening her ears as if she were the most long-suffering animal that had ever lived.

"Do you realize that thing could have turned me into a human iceberg? It could have killed me!"

He took out another can of catfood and furiously opened it, slicing his finger on the lid. He was angry, and shaken, but he was also relieved. After all, the presence hadn't touched him at all. It was looking for Jack Hubbard, not him, but why it should have searched through *his* apartment he couldn't even guess. He didn't have any clothing that belonged to Jack Hubbard, not like Ray, and he didn't have any of his possessions, nothing that might have carried his scent.

Except, of course, his English homework.

He emptied TT's food into her bowl, and it smelled strongly of tuna and chicken livers. How could cats eat that stuff, especially for breakfast? Wrapping a sheet of kitchen towel around his bleeding finger, he went back into the living-room. His briefcase was still in the same place where he had flung it last night, behind the couch, and he picked it up. It wasn't its old dog-eared brown leathery self, it was dark with ice and completely rigid. The lock was frozen solid and he couldn't open it, so he carried it into the kitchen, put it down on the table, and started to chisel off the ice with his potato-peeler. TT kept on greedily eating.

"You don't care, do you?" Jim demanded. "All you care about is that great big overstuffed stomach of yours."

The lock flicked open. Cautiously, he reached inside his briefcase, searching for yesterday's homework. But he couldn't feel any papers at all. He shook the briefcase, and then he tipped it out over the table to see that twenty essays on 'The Ball Poem' had been reduced to nothing but soft, freezing crystals. God knows how cold it must have been inside his briefcase for that to have happened. Two hundred below? Maybe more.

He sifted the crystals through his fingers. This was very frightening. He had already thought that the presence must have an acute sense of smell to be able to detect which water-fountain Jack had drunk from. But to be able to sniff out his scent from a single sheet of paper inside a locked briefcase, that was a sensitivity from which it would be almost impossible for Jack to escape.

No wonder Jack's father had hung his home with Inuit talismans and given Jack an ivory medallion. They were the only way to keep the presence from entering his home and finding him while he slept.

Jim showered and then came out and drank his coffee. He was so tired after his long night tramping the tundra that he needed a caffeine jolt. He was just about to leave for college when Mervyn rapped on the door.

"Jim! You must tell me what you thought about last night! Wasn't I sensational?"

"You were great, Mervyn. No doubt about it. Roberta Flack should eat her heart out."

"Well, *you* don't sound very enthusiastic."

"I do. I am. But I've got trouble at college and it's overspilling into my private life."

"You mean the luscious Karen Goudemark? Everything you said about her was true. She's a peach. She's a peach with strawberry topping and aerosol cream."

"Thanks, Mervyn. But I think that I've scared her off."

"What's scary about you? You're five-eight and your arms look like macaroni."

"Thank you, I needed some extra confidence."

"You need to be strong and forceful. That's what a woman like Karen wants. So what if she's a biologist? She's still a woman. She's not looking for deep or clever or cynical. She's not looking for occult, either. Women don't like occult. And you know what you're like, always babbling on about spirits and werewolves and dead children talking to you by the candy counter in Ralph's."

"I have to go," Jim told him. "Keep an eye on TT for me, will you? There's something real strange about that cat."

"Oh, TT and I understand each other. Don't we, TT?"

TT had finished eating now and had jumped up onto the windowsill, where she sat staring northward, at nothing at all.

"See what I mean? Strange. I mean, what's she looking at?"

Dr Friendly intercepted him as he hurried toward Special Class II. "James! James! A word, please!"

"I know. I'm late again. I dreamed I was on the Trans-Siberian Express with Mrs Friendly and I overslept."

Dr Friendly ignored that quip. Instead, he said, in a highly confidential undertone, "I gather from Madeleine Ouster that she's offered you an educational research position in Washington."

Jim nodded, and spoke just as quietly in reply. "I said that I'd consider it."

"Good. Because what I'd like you to do is, consider it."

"I *am* considering it."

"But consider it very seriously. In fact, consider it so seriously that you take it. It's a great offer, by the sound of it. Once-in-a-lifetime. You'll be able to teach William Faulkner and Herman Melville to dumb gum-chewing illiterate losers all over this great nation of ours, from sea to pollution-ridden sea."

"And what will you do? Close down Special Class Two?"

"Oh, you bet. Not to mention Special Classes One and Three. And that Thursday-evening drama class for kids who have no natural acting ability whatsoever. It's about time the resources that go into those classes went to the students who really deserve them. Who's that black student who always dresses like a bee?"

"Tarquin Tree. Why? He's extremely gifted when it comes to language."

"Oh, really? He's also extremely gifted when it comes to passing wind when he's walking along the corridor right in front of me."

"You mean he farted?"

"You could call it that, if you want to be Rabelaisian about it."

"I'll have him apologize."

"No, thanks. He already did, in what-do-you-call-it, rap. 'Sorry that my gas/ Caused such a fracas'. I can't remember all of it, thank God."

"See what I mean? Gifted."

He was still talking to Dr Friendly when it seemed as a huge dark shadow passed over the college. It was like an eclipse of the sun, or a vast alien spaceship flying overhead. Outside the windows, the sun dimmed, and Jim experienced a distinct shiver of cold. Even Dr Friendly looked around and frowned.

"Did you feel that?" he asked. "It was like somebody walking over my grave."

The temperature in the corridor dropped and dropped and continued to drop; and the day grew darker and darker. The noise from the classrooms suddenly abated, as students became aware of the gloom and the sudden cold. Jim heard shouting from outside the building someplace, and a strange cracking sound, really loud, as if somebody were breaking up timber.

"What the devil's happening?" Dr Friendly exclaimed. "It's an earthquake! Do you think it's an earthquake? Here – we'd better go stand in a doorway!"

But Jim had seen the star pattern in the sky last night and he could guess what it was. "It isn't an earthquake," he told Dr Friendly. "Do you feel the ground moving? No. It's something worse than an earthquake. Call nine one one and ask for everything – fire, paramedics and police."

"Are you out of your mind? Call the emergency services here *again*? Dr Ehrlichman's going to go apeshit!"

"Very beautifully put. Gifted. Now, please. Call them, and tell them it's urgent."

With that, he dropped his briefcase and ran off along the corridor. As he ran, he almost collided with students coming out of their classrooms, clapping their hands together and complaining about the cold.

"Mr Rook!" called out Laura Killmeyer. "What's going on, Mr Rook?"

"Evacuate the class, Laura. All of you, get the hell out. And tell all the other classes to evacuate, too."

"I don't understand. What's happening?"

"If my guess is right, the coldest snap in Southern California since the Ice Age. Now, go! As quick as you can!"

He ran on. As he reached the steps that led up to the double exit doors, he heard more shouting and somebody screaming. The cry was so agonized that he couldn't tell if it was a man or a woman. Then he heard more cracking, much louder this time; and a deep, underlying crunching noise, like something very heavy being dragged over gravel. Pushing his way out on to the patio at the back of the Liberal Arts building, he saw an incredible sight.

The sky above the college was the bruised color of tarnished copper. Out of the sky a very fine shower of ice-particles was falling, so sharp that they prickled his face. The temperature must have been close to fifty degrees below, and everything was frozen – the flowering shrubs, the yuccas, the eucalyptus trees. The brick pathway was already covered with a nubbly coating of slippery ice and the windows in the science building were breaking as their frames contracted, which was causing the cracking, splintering noise.

The outdoor swimming pool was frozen over with rearing pillars of ice. Two students were caught in it – one was frozen up to his shoulders right in the middle, and he was screaming in agony. The other had been just about to lift himself out of the pool and was caught by one ankle: he was Jack Hubbard. At least twenty other students were milling around, shouting and crying and calling out for help. They were wearing only bathing-costumes, and the abrupt drop in temperature must have given them a severe physical shock.

One of the boys was screaming, "There's more of them under the ice! I can see them! They're all trapped under the ice!"

Jim instantly turned around, stumbling on his unglued shoe-sole. He went back through the doors to the glass case where the fire-ax was kept. Smashing the glass with his elbow, he took out the ax and galloped back up the steps, yelling out, "Everybody go in and find your clothes! Do it now! Then evacuate the college!"

He saw Dennis Pease and Christopher L'Ouverture standing close by, and said, "Dennis! Christopher! Are you okay? I need help to get these guys out of here! Go to Clarence's storeroom and bring whatever you can – pickaxes, shovels, anything. And get Clarence here too!"

With that, he jumped down on to the icy surface of the pool and started to make his way toward the student who was trapped up to his shoulders in the middle. Jack called out, "Help me, Mr Rook! I can't move!" but Jim said, "You'll have to wait a couple of minutes! This guy needs me more!"

He half-ran, half-slid to the student in the middle. The boy had stopped screaming now, and he was choking for breath. It was Waylon Price, his face blueish black from suffocation. In the same way that pack ice had crushed the ships of so many Arctic explorers, Waylon was being gradually compressed – his ribs breaking, his lungs constricted.

Waylon stared at Jim with bulging eyes. "*Others*," he gasped. "Others, underneath. I felt them pull my feet."

Jim frantically used the side of his hand to rub away the opaque ice particles from the surface of the pool. He bent his head downward, and shaded his eyes with his hand, and to his horror he could see at least four or five shadowy shapes struggling in the milky-colored water below. There must have been a narrow air-pocket directly beneath the ice, because they kept bobbing upward and pressing their desperate faces upward. He thought he saw Suzie Wintz down there – he recognized her new red gingham swimsuit – and Mandy Saintskill, too. In this temperature they wouldn't last longer than a couple of minutes.

"Shut your eyes, Waylon," Jim told him, and lifted the ax. His first blow did no more than chip off a thin triangular piece of ice. But he struck again, and again, and with each blow he became more and more angry at what had happened to his students. They were freezing, they were drowning, they were dying, and all that Dr Friendly would think was that they were dumb gum-chewing no-hopers and that the world was probably better off without them.

Jim gripped the ax in both hands and hacked at the ice in front of Waylon's chest. It was even thicker than it looked from the surface, but at last he managed to break off a sizeable lump, and heave it out of the water, and then another. Then he was able to kick away bigger and bigger lumps with his feet.

More teachers had arrived now, and Clarence, too. They gathered round and lifted Waylon out of the water, while others knelt beside the broken hole in the ice and grasped the hands of the students who had been trapped underneath. One by one they brought them out of the freezing water, white with cold, their eyes as scarlet as zombies. They were helped or carried to the edge of the pool where blankets and stretchers were waiting for them. At the same time, Jim heard the sound of sirens. The paramedics were here again.

Clarence was breaking free the ice from Jack's ankle. Jim was quickly making a head count of all of his students. They all seemed to be there, but where was that red gingham swimsuit?

"Is Suzie Wintz there?" he shouted. "She's wearing a red swimsuit, checkered!"

"Not here!" Mr Davies shouted back. "Maybe they've taken her inside!"

Jim thought: *oh, no, not Suzie* and peered back into the hole in the ice. He couldn't see anything at all but the gelid, chlorinated water. Maybe they had lifted her out, but he couldn't remember seeing her. Jesus, what if she's still down there, trapped under the ice, breathing from an air-pocket and waiting for somebody to rescue her?

Mr Davies was walking across the ice toward him. "I've sent one of the boys to see if they took her to the infirmary."

"Too late," said Jim. "We don't have the time."

"What?"

Without another word, Jim held his nose and jumped into the water. He knew it was cold, but he hadn't been prepared to have all the air knocked out of his lungs. He gasped and struggled and floundered around, and at last he managed to kick his way up to the surface again. He spouted out water and took three deep breaths.

"Jim, come out of there!" yelled Mr Davies, reaching out his hand. "It's too damn cold, you'll be frozen to death!"

"Mr Rook, the firemen are coming!" said Clarence. "You don't have to take such a risky chance!"

Jim took another deep breath, shook his head, and dived under the water again. He swam around in a circle, trying to catch a glimpse of red gingham through the freezing murk.

Through the water, he could hear the clonking sound of bubbles, and people walking on the ice above his head, and somebody trying to hack the sides of the hole to make it bigger. He hoped that he could remember where the hole was. Everything looked the same down here: a dim pearly world beneath a white, cave-like ceiling.

He began to realize that his lungs were aching. Not only that, his arms and legs were growing numb, and he was finding it more and more difficult to make them go through the motions of swimming. He knew that he would have to go up for more air, and that he wouldn't have the strength to come back down again.

Just as he turned around, he suddenly bumped into something soft and pale and cold. He almost gasped in shock. It was Suzie Wintz, her blonde hair floating around her in a halo, her eyes wide open, staring at him through the water from only inches away.

He knew that he was risking his own life to try to get her back up to the surface. But people who drowned in very cold water had a chance, didn't they, if the paramedics could get their hearts beating soon enough?

He seized her, and held her under his left arm, and struck for the surface. His head pounded and his back muscles ached and he couldn't even feel his hands and his feet. He had forgotten where the hole in the ice was and he didn't think that he was going to make it. But at least they wouldn't be able to say that he hadn't tried. That was the whole point, trying. And Dr Friendly would shed a tear at his funeral and secretly smile because that would the end of Special Class II.

The thought of that gave him a last burst of energy. He kicked his legs and flapped his one free arm and then miraculously he broke the surface. Strong, eager hands dragged them both out.

"Get her heart started!" Jim shouted out, his teeth chattering so much that he was barely intelligible. "She's precious!
Don't let her die! Get her heart started!"

A woman paramedic wrapped him in a blanket and led
him toward the edge of the pool, where a gurney was
waiting. It was Rachel, the red-haired woman who had
amputated Ray Krueger's hands. "Lie down," she said,
gently. "We'll soon have you warmed up again."

"I don't want to lie down. I need to make sure that
Suzie's okay."

"They're working on her now. I'll tell you as soon as
there's any news."

The ambulance abruptly whooped its siren, and bounced
off across the grass, taking Suzie with it. Jim sat on the
small wall beside the swimming-pool but he wouldn't lie
down. Dr Ehrlichman came up to him and laid his hand on
his shoulder. "I just want to tell you that was a very brave
thing you did, going in for Suzie like that."

"Don't let him break up the class, will you?" Jim
shivered.

"I'm sorry, I don't understand."

"It doesn't matter. I'm a little upset, that's all."

Dr Ehrlichman patted his shoulder again. "Quite under-
standable. You just take care of yourself."

The coppery sky began to lighten, and gradually the
sun came through. With surprising rapidity, the ice on
the surface of the pool began to melt, and within twenty
minutes there were only a few large lumps of it left,
slowly circling around in the sunshine. Jim saw Rachel
the paramedic talking to Karen, and eventually Karen came
across and sat down next to him.

"You need to change into something dry. Do you want
me to drive you home?"

"I'm waiting to hear about Suzie."

"I know that. But the paramedics have promised to call my mobile."

Jim suddenly felt very tired. He nodded, and said, "Okay . . . why don't you take me home? I feel like a goddamned snowman, sitting here."

As they walked toward the parking-lot, Lieutenant Harris appeared, looking as hot and sweaty as ever.

"They told me the pool froze over."

"That's right."

"Any ideas how it might have happened?"

"Winter came early, I guess."

Lieutenant Harris folded his notebook and shoved it back into his pocket. "Yeah, that's what I thought. Merry Christmas, Mr Rook."

Karen drove him home and came up to his apartment with him. TT greeted her with her usual suspicion, but Karen stroked her chin and that seemed to appease her. She jumped up on to the back of the couch and resumed her vigil on the windowsill.

"That's a very strange cat," said Karen. "She almost seems to think that she's human."

"In some ways, I guess. But no human would eat what she eats."

"Do you want me to make you some coffee? You're looking kind of pale."

"That would be good, thanks. I'm just going to change into something dry."

Karen went into the kitchen and filled up the espresso machine. "I guess I have to eat my words, don't I?" she called.

"About what?"

"About the stars we saw. They *were* an omen, weren't they?"

"Yes, I think they were. And this isn't over yet. We're going to suffer more and more sudden freezes like this; and they're going to get worse; and more students are going to be hurt."

"So what can we do about it? We have to do something."

Jim came into the kitchen, tucking a crumpled white T-shirt into his jeans. "If I knew what it was that I was looking for, it would make things a whole lot easier. But this is invisible, unpredictable, and it may be completely imaginary. For all I know, we could still put these incidents down to some kind of freakish weather conditions."

"So why don't you call in a meteorologist?"

Jim didn't have time to answer before the phone rang. He picked it up and said, "Jim Rook."

"James, this is Dr Friendly. I've just had word from the hospital and I thought you ought to be the first to know. They took Suzie Wintz off the life-support machine about fifteen minutes ago, with the consent of her parents. I'm sorry, James. I truly am. I admire what you did to save her and I know that you're going to be deeply grieved."

Jim hung up without saying a word. Karen stared at him and said, "What is it? Not Suzie Wintz?"

He nodded. He felt utterly stunned. But he also felt a rising anger, too. Nobody was going to maim and kill his students, nobody. And he was going to do whatever it took to stop it happening, now.

Ten

H e hammered on the door of Henry Hubbard's apartment like a man hammering on the door of hell. After a few moments Henry Hubbard opened it, looking shocked. Jim pushed past him into his apartment and went straight into the living-room. Jack was there, too, sitting on the couch with a brightly colored woven blanket wrapped round his shoulders. He lifted his head and blinked at Jim in bewilderment.

"Mr Rook?"

Jim said, "Suzie Wintz is dead."

"Oh, no. I'm so sorry. Oh, God."

"Who's Suzie Wintz?" asked Henry Hubbard.

"A classmate of Jack's. A young girl of nineteen years old from a broken family background with very little chance of ever becoming very much more than a cocktail waitress or somebody's beaten wife. She drowned today when the college pool froze over. We thought that we could maybe save her but we couldn't."

"I don't know what to say," said Henry Hubbard.

"Oh, but that's not true. You know exactly what to say. You know why that pool froze over, just like you know why that handrail froze up, and the washroom was all iced up. There's something here and it's looking for Jack and it freezes everything that feels like Jack or smells like Jack. It wants him, and I want to know why."

Henry Hubbard turned his face away. "I can't tell you that."

Jim went up to him and grabbed his shirt and stared him fiercely in the eye. "A girl died today, Mr Hubbard. A young boy has lost both of his arms. Whatever this thing is, it's going to get Jack in the end, and then what will you say to me? 'No comment'? 'I can't tell you that'?"

Henry Hubbard took a deep breath. Then he said, "Jack . . . why don't you leave us for a moment?"

"No," said Jim. "He's one of my students too. If you have anything to say that directly concerns him, I think he has a right to hear it, don't you?"

Henry Hubbard sat down in one of the armchairs. He lowered his head for a while. Then he said, "Very well. You don't give me much choice, do you?"

"This is not about choice. This is about survival."

"Well, yes. You're exactly right. It *is* about survival. I never really believed that it would come to this. But now that it has . . . I'm afraid that I don't really know what to do about it, how to stop it. That sounds pretty damned feeble, doesn't it? But sometimes life throws you a problem and you simply don't have the wherewithal to deal with it. The faith, or whatever it takes."

He sat down. Jack was staring at him as if he had never seen him before – as if he had just discovered that his father was a total stranger.

Jim said quietly, "What really happened in Alaska, Mr Hubbard?"

"It was the worst blizzard that any of us had ever experienced. The winds were so strong that most of the time we could barely stand up straight. It was no use hoping that anybody would come to pull us out of there. The weather was far too severe for an airplane or a helicopter.

"On the third day Randy fell down a rocky slope and broke

his ankle. I strapped it up and we took it in turns to help him hobble along. But after nine hours we were all exhausted and Randy was in too much pain to go on. We decided that we'd pitch our tent and that Randy and Charles would stay there together while I went on to find help.

"I walked through that blizzard for a whole day. We had all experienced the feeling that a 'fourth man' was with us, but now that I was on my own I started to see it more clearly, and closer. A tall figure in a white hooded robe, carrying a long staff. It was always off to my left, and slightly ahead of me, so that I could never see its face.

"Once or twice I shouted out to it, but it never showed any signs of hearing me. If I stopped for a rest it went striding on and disappeared into the snow, but when I started walking again he reappeared. It frightened me, but at the same time it reassured me, too, because I thought that it must know where it was going, and that as long as I followed it I had a chance of survival.

"Of course I didn't have the video camera with me now, so I couldn't take any pictures of it. That's why I've been looking at the video footage so hard . . . to make sure that it was real, and that it wasn't just an hallucination. Sometimes I think I can see it, but then I rerun the video and look again and it was only a flurry of snow."

"So what happened?" asked Jim. "Did it guide you out of there?"

Henry Hubbard took a deep breath. "By the time it started to grow dark, I still hadn't reached any trading posts or settlements and I still couldn't see any landmarks. I was expecting to come across the Sheenjek Glacier, which would have showed me the way south to Fort Despair. But the terrain was all the same, mile after mile, and none of my navigational equipment was working. I didn't have a tent. The ground was so frozen so hard that it would taken all night to dig myself any kind of shelter. I kept on walking but I didn't know where I was going and I was quite certain then that I was going to die.

"They say that when you're dying of exhaustion and hyopthermia you reach a point where all you want to do is lie down and let the snow cover you and go to sleep. But I didn't feel that at all. I felt angry. I felt angry because everything had gone so badly wrong, and the weather had been so severe, and because I was going to die so young and never see my son again. I railed against God, if you must know, for letting me down. Hadn't I always prayed? Hadn't I always believed in Him? And so where was He now – now that I really needed Him?

"I collapsed on to my knees. I couldn't walk any further. It was then that I saw the figure standing not far away, quite still. I dropped my flashlight and when I managed to pick it up the figure was standing even closer, so close that I could have touched it. Although the wind was blowing so hard, its robe didn't stir at all. It was brilliant white, with a kind of soft white halo of light all around it. I couldn't tell if it was a man or a woman. I couldn't even tell if it was human. Its face was completely hidden inside its hood.

"It stood beside me without moving for – I don't know – maybe it was only ten minutes but it seemed like hours. Then I said, 'Can you help me? Are you here to help me or are you just going to watch me die?'

"For a long, long time it didn't say anything at all. Then it spoke to me. It's very hard to describe its voice, but I won't ever forget it for as long as I live. It was like thin ice cracking, that's all I can say. It could have been either a man or a woman, I couldn't tell. It had an accent of some kind but I don't have any idea what it was. It said, 'You didn't come here to die, did you? You came here looking for glory.'

"I don't think that I have ever been so frightened in my life. There was something about it, that figure. Its presence was so cold that it made the blizzard seem warm, by comparison. At least the blizzard was alive, howling and shrieking and full of whirling snow. But this figure, this was something else. If I didn't know better, I'd say it was Death. You know, Death with a capital 'D'. The Grim Reaper, in person.

"I shouted at it. Well, I had to shout, to make myself heard. I said, 'I'm not interested in glory any more. I want to live, that's all! I want to survive!'

"The figure was silent for a while. Then it said, 'How much do you wish to survive? What will you give me, in return for your life? Will you give me the thing that it is dearest to you?'

"I said—" and here Henry Hubbard had to stop, overwhelmed with the memory of what had happened, overwhelmed with what he had done.

"You said what, Mr Hubbard?" Jim coaxed him.

Henry Hubbard lifted his eyes in a look of utter despair. "I said it could have anything at all, so long as I survived. You see, I didn't really believe that it was real. I thought it was something inside of my head. Not an hallucination exactly, or a mirage, but a kind of external projection of my survival instincts, to help me think more rationally about how I was going to get out of this situation.

"I said it could have everything I owned. Everything. But it said, 'What do I want with possessions, here in the cold? I want warmth. I want the warmth of a human soul.' I said that I didn't understand. What soul? And that's when it said, 'I want you son. I will let you live, in exchange for the soul of your son.'"

Henry Hubbard's eyes filled with tears. "That's when I was sure that it wasn't real. Because how could a figure in the middle of Alaska know that I had a son? That's when I was sure that it was my own mind playing tricks on me. So I said, yes. You can have my son's soul, and anything else you want, but just let me get out of here alive."

"You offered it my *soul*?" said Jack, incredulously. "You're my father! You offered it my *soul*?"

Henry Hubbard nodded. "I don't have any excuses, Jack, except that I was still convinced that I was hallucinating. The figure said, 'Be assured that I will keep you to that promise. Others have tried to renege on their agreements with me, and they have come to regret it.' I mean, for God's sake, here was this tall mysterious figure in the middle of a blizzard and it was talking like my lawyer. I *had* to be hallucinating."

"But you weren't," said Jim.

"No. The figure knelt down beside me in the snow and said, 'Climb on my back.'

"At first I didn't want to, but it stayed where it was, waiting for me, and in the end I put my arms around its neck and climbed on to its back. I could feel its body through its robes: it was bony, as if it had hardly any flesh on it at all. But it hefted me up, and put its arms under my thighs to stop me from sliding off, the way you do with your kids, and it began to walk.

"I felt unsafe and desperately uncomfortable, and I couldn't stand the feeling of its shoulder bones, but I was too exhausted to have any choice. The figure kept on walking through the blizzard and after a while the joggling began to send me to sleep. I tried not to close my eyes but I couldn't help it. All I could hear was the wind screaming and the snow pattering against my face and the crunch, crunch, crunch of the figure's feet, as it kept on walking.

"I must have slept for hours. I woke up in the morning to find myself lying in the snow outside a small Inuit trading-post called Anatuk. The wind had died down and the sun was shining. An Inuit woman came out of the trading-post and saw me, and called her husband. They helped me inside, and the rest you know."

"You didn't see the figure, or any sign of it?"

"I saw footprints, leading to the place where I was lying. But there was only one set of them, so I told myself that they had to be mine."

"The figure was carrying you, remember."

"I know. And the footprints were larger than mine. But it was a warm morning, by Arctic Circle standards, and the footprints had already thawed out some, which could have accounted for that. When they melt, footprints always look much bigger. That's why some people think they've come across Abominable Snowman tracks, when they're probably only rabbit spoor."

"So you decided that it had all been a dream, and that the figure hadn't really existed?"

"Well, what would you have thought, if the same thing had happened to you?"

"I don't know. Maybe I'm less of a skeptic than you are."

Henry Hubbard said, "Ralph and Charles were found dead at about three o'clock that afternoon. Their tent had blown away during the night, and they hadn't stood a chance. I was devastated. They were both such good men. But I guess that was the first time that I began to have suspicions that I might not have been hallucinating, after all. Their bodies were found at the foot of Hungry Horse Pass, which is over a hundred and thirty-eight miles to the south-east of Anatuk. Even the fittest man in the world couldn't walk a hundred and thirty-eight miles in a sixty-five miles per hour blizzard in the middle of the night."

"Did you tell anybody?"

Henry Hubbard shook his head. "I told a deliberate lie,

and said that I had left them a day earlier than I really had. I have a reputation in this business, Mr Rook. Everybody would have asked how I managed to travel so far in a single night. The only logical conclusion would have been that a trapper had come across me and given me a ride to Anatuk by snowmobile. In which case, why hadn't I made any effort to go back for my two companions? But if I insisted that some kind of snow creature rescued me by carrying me on its back, everybody would have said that I was raving. So that was the choice I had. And that was why I said nothing."

"That washroom incident, was that the first inclination you had that the snowman might be searching for Jack?"

"No. I hadn't wanted to leave Anchorage so soon, because I needed some time to recover from the expedition, physically and mentally. Apart from that I still had some extra interviews and local footage to shoot. We had an apartment on Northern Lights Boulevard, overlooking Westchester Lagoon. A great place, we both loved it. But I kept having dreams about the figure in the snow. Night after night. And every night I could hear it whispering to me in that voice like crackling ice: '*Remember what you promised.*'

"Then one day I came back home after only about a half-hour at the sound recording studio. I'd forgotten some of my notes. Jack had left for college – probably not more than ten minutes before, because the toaster was still warm. I checked his bedroom and I was annoyed to see that he hadn't made his bed. But then it realized that it was freezing cold in there, and that his bed was sparkling.

"It was frozen solid. You know what sheets are like when you leave them on the line on a winter's day? You could have cracked these like cuttlefish shells. The whole bed was rock-hard, even his pajamas."

"That's when you knew that you hadn't been hallucinating after all?"

Henry Hubbard said, "That's when I went to talk to my late wife's father. He told me that there were dozens of stories about the Snowman. It craves human companionship, which is why it accompanies parties of explorers across the ice. It was supposed to have been a kind of angel, privileged to sit on the right-hand side of the Great Immortal Being who created the world. But when the Great Immortal Being made the Inuit people, the angel became fiercely jealous. He had given them souls, and the angel – being an angel – had no soul. One day, one of the Great Immortal Being's favorite humans, the hunter Ninavut, was caught in a snowstorm. The angel deliberately misled him deeper and deeper into the storm and his sled fell through thin ice and he drowned. When the Great Immortal Being found out what had happened, He was so angry that He took away the angel's eyes, and banished it to the coldest parts of the earth, the north and south poles. He was never to sit or walk on the right side of one of the Great Immortal Being or one of his creations ever again; and he was charged with the task of rescuing any human whom he found in trouble.

"The angel begged for mercy, but the Great Immortal Being was adamant. However, He softened His heart enough to allow the angel to exact whatever price he wanted for carrying out the rescue. If ever the Great Immortal Being made a mistake, that was it. Ever since that day, the angel accompanied every party of Arctic explorers across the ice. It's taking care of them, as the Great Immortal Being commanded it, but at the same time it is hungrily waiting for them to get into difficulty, so that it can save them, and ask for an exorbitant price in return.

"That price is always a human soul. The Snowman breathes it in, and the soul gives it a few hours' comforting warmth, and makes it feel for a while that it's one of the Great Immortal Being's favored creations."

Graham Masterton

Henry Hubbard turned to Jack and said, "I was delirious, almost frozen to death. If I'd have thought for one moment that the Snowman was real, that it was capable of coming after you – I would have laid down in the snow and given myself up to the blizzard. Anything, rather than harm you.

"I even asked your grandfather if it was possible for the bargain to be changed . . . if I could give the Snowman my soul instead of yours. But he said that it was impossible. The Snowman had been duty-bound by the Great Immortal Being to save my life and to protect me for ever."

Jack stood up. "You're my father, and you offered my soul to some goddamned ice monster? How could you have done that – even if you *were* delirious?"

"Jack, I simply didn't believe it was real."

"If you didn't believe it was real, how did you think it was going to save you?"

"I don't know. It was fifty degrees below, Jack. I wasn't thinking straight."

"Straight enough to condemn your only son to death, just to save your ass. And now look what's happened. Suzie's dead and Ray might just as well be dead, too. And that thing's still coming after me."

Henry Hubbard lowered his head. "I guess there's no point in saying sorry."

"None at all, Dad," snapped Jack, and walked out of the room, leaving the door wide open.

Jim waited for a moment and then he said, "We're going to have to find some way of beating this Snowman, Mr Hubbard. I can't have any more of my students hurt, and that includes Jack."

"My father-in-law said that the Inuit won't ever try, because the Snowman's fate was decreed by the Great Immortal Being. If they attempted to harm it, that would be a direct affront to their creator. But the man who built

Dead Man's Mansion, Edward Grace, told his Inuit friends that he had devised a way to hunt it down and destroy it. Apparently that was one of the reasons he died . . . his Inuit friends no longer brought him oil and supplies because they thought he was going to commit a terrible crime against their beliefs."

"He had actually found a way of licking this thing? Do you know that for a fact?"

"There are no facts north of the Arctic Circle, Mr Rook, apart from the thermometer. In conditions of extreme cold, all kinds of irrational things happen. Even the basic elements behave in ways that you can't believe. Robert Peary saw an entire range of mountains in the Arctic, and called them Crocker Land, and in 1913 Donald MacMillan sent an expedition to look for them. He saw them, but as soon as the sun went down they disappeared, and there was nothing but a vast plain of ice for as far as the eye could see. A mirage, Mr Rook. And it's quite possible that Dead Man's Mansion is nothing but a mirage, or a myth. Up in Alaska, it's almost impossible to seperate reality from legend."

"If Edward Grace *had* found a way, though, there might be some evidence of it, up in his house? If his playing cards were still intact after all that time, who's to say that he doesn't have papers, or notebooks, or diaries, something like that?"

"A very slim chance, I'd say."

"Slim, yes. But still a chance."

Henry Hubbard tiredly rubbed the back of his neck. "You'd have to find the house first. There must have been dozens of expeditions over the years, but apart from one or two chance sightings, nobody knows exactly where it is."

"You'd help me find it, though, wouldn't you?"

"*You*? You're not serious, are you? Do you have any idea what kind of terrain we're talking about? What kind of conditions? You have to be one hundred per cent fit, with years of experience in trekking and climbing and survival techniques."

"I don't trek, but I *schelp* down to the liquor store now and again. And I used to climb into my old apartment all the time, when I'd forgotten my key. As for survival . . . I teach Special Class Two, Mr Hubbard, and anybody who can survive that can survive anything."

"It's impossible."

"It's not impossible. Nothing is impossible, so far as protecting my students is concerned. If finding Dead Man's Mansion offers them some kind of a chance, then I'm going to go find Dead Man's Mansion. I don't care whether you come with me or not, but since you have the know-how, it would probably make things a whole lot easier."

"Mr Rook, I don't think you have any idea what you're proposing to do."

"You're right. I don't. But I'm going to do it all the same."

"You realize that you'll probably die."

Jim said, "I'm talking about the lives of nearly twenty young people here. Including your own son."

Henry Hubbard looked away. "I'm not sure that I can face going back to Alaska, Mr Rook. That creature robbed me of all the nerve I ever had."

"Listen, my students feel like that sometimes, when they're faced with an English test."

"There's a hell of a difference between taking an English test and crossing the Sheenjek glacier."

"No there isn't, if it frightens you just as much. I have a severely dyslexic girl in my class. She's nineteen years old and she still can't make a rhyme or recite the days of the week. Do you know what she said to me the other day? She said that English tests made her feel physically sick and that sometimes she felt she would rather take an overdose than have to show up for class to take another one.

"So I let her take it a step at a time. I encourage her to plan what she's going to do, and make one success out of a series of small successes."

"Mr Rook, you don't tackle an Arctic exploration as a series of small successes. Either you succeed totally or you die. Alaska isn't a land of half-measures."

Jim was silent for a long time. Then he said, "That's how we're going to leave it, is it? You're just going to sit here feeling sorry for yourself while this Snowman creature tracks Jack down and freezes him to death?"

Henry Hubbard didn't reply for so long that Jim thought that he was never going to. Eventually, however, he stood up and said: "It's going to take money. We're going to need clothing, equipment, transponders; and we'll have to rent a snowmobile."

"I have a couple of thousand in my savings account."

"Well, that'll help. The TV producers have already paid me twenty-two thousand; and my wife left a little when she died."

"Does this mean you'll do it?"

Henry Hubbard gave him the haunted look of a soldier who knows that he has to go back to the Front. "When it comes down to it, I don't really have a choice, do I?"

Eleven

That afternoon, Dr Friendly rapped on his classroom door and said, "Sorry to interrupt, James. But there's a phone call for you. Madeleine Ouster."

Jim told his class to continue reading from *The Lost Boy* and followed Dr Friendly down the corridor to the principal's office. There were at least fifteen police officers and six or seven forensic investigators milling around in the college lobby, along with reporters and two TV crews. West Grove's frozen swimming pool had made news all around the world, and meteorological experts from five different countries had come up with wildly differing opinions as to how the phenomenon had occurred.

Two or three reporters came hurrying up to Jim, asking him for quotes. "How do you feel about the tragedy today, Mr Rook?" "How are Suzie's fellow students coping?" "Some TV preachers are saying that this was a sign from God to bring Bible study back into our colleges, what do you say?"

Jim waved them away and went into Dr Ehrlichman's office and closed the door. Dr Friendly held out the phone and said, "This is your big chance here, James."

"Mr Rook? This is Madeline Ouster. I'm leaving for Washington in a half-hour and I was very disappointed not to hear from you this morning."

"I'm sorry, that was discourteous of me. I was kind of tied up with this swimming-pool business."

"I was very sad to hear about that. I hope you'll accept my condolences. I also hope that you'll accept my offer of a job."

Jim said, "I've thought it over very carefully, Ms Ouster. But I'm afraid that I have to think of my commitment to my class."

"I know you're a very loyal teacher, Mr Rook. But think about this on a national level. The needs of the many far outweigh the needs of the few."

"Didn't Mr Spock say that?"

"Whoever said it, Mr Rook, they were wise words. There are millions of American students who desperately need the kind of enthusiasm for language and literature that you have the gift to inspire."

"Well, I'm very flattered. Don't think that I'm not. But I have a crisis to deal with here, and Special Class Two really need me. So I'm going to have to say thanks, but no thanks."

"I could enhance your salary and pensions package."

"In my dictionary, Ms Ouster, to enhance anything means to increase its beauty. And it would not be very beautiful of me to leave twenty young people right when they need me the most."

Dr Friendly had been listening to this conversation with mounting frustration. *"You can't turn her down!"* he spluttered. *"Don't you realize with a fantastic opportunity she's offering you?"*

"I'm sorry, Ms Ouster," said Jim. "I didn't quite catch that. The coffee was just starting to perk."

Madeleine Ouster said, "I wish you well, Mr Rook, that's all I can say. I personally think that your sense of commitment is a little misguided, but I admire you for it, all the same."

Jim hung up. Dr Friendly stood staring at him in disbelief. "How could you do that?" he demanded.

"Because Suzie Wintz is dead and I don't want the same thing to happen to any more of my students."

"And what, precisely, does Suzie Wintz's death have to do with your turning down a very exciting and lucrative position in Washington?"

"I can't tell you, I'm afraid; and you probably wouldn't believe me, even if I did."

Dr Friendly took a few tight breaths to steady himself. "This won't stop me from rationalizing the special education department, believe me."

"Rationalizing?" That's a good word for abandoning the needs of hundreds of kids who might never be given another chance to learn how to communicate."

"Oh, they know how to communicate all right. I've heard them. They have the widest vocabulary of slang, obscenity and assorted grunts that I've ever come across outside of the Marine Corps."

"I didn't know you were a Marine. Maybe I should have guessed. You do have a certain gung-ho attitude when it comes to teaching English."

"I was in charge of drafting orders, if you must know."

Jim said, "That figures." But then he laid his hand on Dr Friendly's shoulder and said, "Sorry. I'm a little wired, that's all. I want to ask you a favor. I have two weeks' vacation time still owing to me, and I was wondering if I could take it on Monday."

"On *Monday*? This coming Monday?"

"That's the one. I've already talked to Mrs Sennehauer and she's agreed to take over Special Class Two until I get back."

"I don't know how I tolerate you, James. I truly don't."

Snowman

"You tolerate me because you're trying to live up to your name, that's all. Friendly by name, friendly by nature."

As he left college that evening, he saw a group of his students in the parking-lot, talking quietly together. They had all been subdued since Suzie died, but he could see that they were giving each other tremendous support and affection, as if they were all members of the same family. Laura Killmeyer was there with her mirror, as well as Dottie Osias, draped in a black fringed shawl, Christophe l'Ouverture and Tarquin Tree.

He gave them a high-five and walked over to his car. He climbed into the driver's seat and started the engine. At that moment, an orange dropped out of the tree above him and landed on the passenger seat. He picked it up, ready to toss it out, when he realized that it was ice-cold, and hard as a baseball, and that its surface sparkled with frost. He looked up. The orange tree under which he had parked was glittering with white rime. Just like the orange, it was frozen solid.

Jim valuted out of his car, looking around him in all directions. From the rear of the car, he could make out a faint track of sparkling footprints, already melting in the sun. They crossed the parking-lot and headed toward the grassy bank that led to the back of the science block. He saw a quick, furtive moment beneath the trees, but when he shaded his eyes against the sun and stared at it more intently, he realized that it was nothing more than a flicker of sunlight through the branches.

"Laura!' he called. 'Laura, bring me that mirror!"

"What?"

"Bring me that mirror, quick!"

Laura came over, carrying the mirror. "What's the matter, Mr Rook? You look like you've seen a ghost."

"The point is that I *haven't* seen a ghost. But it could

be here. Do you think you might be able to see it in the mirror?"

"I don't know. You'd have to perform the ritual."

"You mean I have to eat half an apple facing east and the other half facing west? I don't have an apple. Do you have an apple?"

"That's only for people you love. If you want to see a spirit you hate, all you have to do is spit once at every point of the compass. Then you have to spit on the mirror and say, *'Mirror, mirror, with this bile; reveal to me the spirit vile.'*"

"And then I'll see it?"

She looked at him with deep earnestness in her eyes. "You should do, if you really believe."

Jim said, "North, which is north?"

"That way, I guess."

He turned around and tried to spit, but his mouth was too dry. "Here," he said to Christophe l'Ouverture, "give me a swig of that Seven Up."

"Say what?" asked Christophe.

"I said, give me a swig of that Seven Up; and make it snappy. I'm all out of spit here and I'm trying to track down an evil spirit."

"I've been drinking out of the bottle, Mr Rook. And, you know—"

"For crying out loud." Jim snatched the bottle of Seven Up out of his hand and took a huge effervescent mouthful. It wasn't just Seven Up, though, it was fifty per cent Bacardi. It burned down his throat and fizzed up his nose and he coughed and coughed and in the end he had to lean against his car, trying to get his breath back.

"Jesus," he said. "You could have warned me."

"Yeah? And get myself busted for breaking college rules?"

"Forget the rules," Jim told him.

He bent forward and spat to the north. Then he spat to all of the other points on the compass. Laura Killmeyer held up the mirror so that he could see his own face, strained and tired and wavering like a character in a 1960s *cinema-verité* movie. "Spit," she said. "I can wipe it off afterward."

He spat, and his saliva trickled down the mirror. Laura touched her hand to her forehead and whispered, "Repeat after me, *'Mirror, mirror, with this bile; reveal to me the spirit vile.'*"

Jim repeated the incantation word for word. "Will it work now? Will I be able to see it?"

"It depends how much you believe."

"Believe me, I believe."

"Then take the mirror for yourself, and look."

Laura handed the mirror over. It was surprisingly light, almost as if it were nothing but an oval of reflective air. "It used to belong to my great-grandmother. She had it hanging in her hallway in New Orleans, but always facing the wall. She said that if she hung it outward, it would capture the souls of everybody who stepped over her threshold, and she didn't want the responsibility for that."

"So why did she hang it there at all?"

"I don't know. But she always used to say that she didn't want a mirror full of souls. She had eleven children. What would she do with a mirror full of souls?"

While they were talking, Jim was slowly panning the mirror from one side of the parking-lot to the other, searching for any trace of the hooded Snowman in white. He couldn't see anything to begin with, just a collection of jumbled visions. Dr Ehrlichman, shaking hands with George Hepplewhite from the college fund-raising committee; the roof of the arts block; the steps that led to the college main entrance; Linda Starewsky in a very short skirt and a tight white T-shirt, walking down to the sport stadium, chewing gum. Three quail, fluttering past.

Then he managed to angle the mirror toward the trees, where the sunlight was dancing through the leaves. At first he couldn't see anything clearly, there were too many harlequin patterns of sun and shadow. But then, deep in the shadow, he saw something standing upright against the trunk of a birch tree, slightly to the right of the main stand of trees. The silvery bark effectively camoflaged it, because its robes were equally pale and silvery, and the darkness of its face could have been a hollow in the trunk.

Jim stared at it in silence, not knowing what to do next. The figure remained where it was, as if it were watching him, and because he knew it was blind, its watchfulness somehow made it even more frightening. What was even more disturbing was that he could see it only if it was behind his back, and he had a sudden surge of dread that it was going to come rushing up to him. If he turned around, it would vanish, and he would be left helpless.

The Snowman was much taller than Jim had imagined, and its shoulders were like the arms of a rocking-chair, covered with a sheet. Jim guessed that it shoulders needed to be wide, if it really carried stranded explorers for miles and miles across the Arctic tundra. But all the same, there was something frighteningly out of proportion about it. Its arms were unusually long, and the shape of its hood suggested that it had a huge and bony head. It carried a tall staff, with which it endlessly prodded and poked at the ground all around it.

The wind restlessly stirred its robes, and there was a lack of clarity about it, a lack of focus. It wavered and danced like a poor television picture.

Even from a distance, the Snowman gave off a deep chill of undiluted malevolence. It smoked with cold. Blind, invisible, and insatiably hungry for the soul that Henry Hubbard had promised it.

"You can *see* it, Mr Rook?" asked Laura.

Jim nodded. "I can see it all right. It's . . . I don't know. It's very weird. Very scary."

"Let me look."

Jim titled the mirror away. "Laura – this is something you really don't want to see, believe me."

"Oh, come on. I'm a witch. I'm not scared of spirits."

"Laura, this isn't like seeing your dead grandma or the boy that you're going to marry. This is the same thing that killed Suzie and froze Ray's hands. It's real and it's only about a hundred feet away."

"*Please* let me look."

He shook his head. "I'm sorry. I can't have you involved in this. You or any other student."

He directed the mirror back toward the trees, but the figure had disappeared. Anxiously, he twisted it from left to right, but there was no sign of the Snowman anywhere at all.

"God damn it," he swore. He took the mirror and walked toward the trees, until he came to the place by the silver birch where the Snowman had been standing. Again he swiveled the mirror around, and for an instant he thought he saw a white flicker, as if the Snowman had turned the corner by the gymnasium, but it could have been nothing more than a breeze-blown fragment of paper.

Laura caught up with him. "I could help you," she insisted. "I really know magic, and this is magic, isn't it? Kind of magic, anyhow."

Jim handed her the mirror and knelt down on the ground. Underneath the silver birch tree, the grass was frozen into razor-sharp spikes. "Look at this," he said. "This thing freezes everything it touches."

155

He stood up, looked around a few moments more, and then walked back toward his car, with Laura following him.

"There are all kinds of spells to ward off the cold," she said. "There's an incredible spell that old *babushkas* used to cast in Russia, to revive people who had frozen to death. You boil three live rats, two pounds of butter and five hot peppers in a samovar."

"This isn't just cold we're talking about here," said Jim. "This thing freezes the sidewalk wherever it walks, even in eighty-degree heat. It can freeze catfood in the can. It can freeze paper into dust. He picked up the orange which had dropped into his car, and threw it against the ground. It shattered into tiny frozen fragments, as if it were made of bright orange glass. "It can freeze a human being the same way. You want that to happen to you?"

"There's a spell that the Sherpas used to use in Nepal, to destroy the ice-demons which they thought were killing their goats."

"Boy, you really know your magic, don't you?"

"They used fire," Laura insisted. "You can always kill an ice-demon by setting it alight."

"It's that easy?"

"No, it's not that easy. You can light a fire but you can't force the spirit to walk into it. It has to burn itself voluntarily. In other words, you have to find a way of making the fire seem like the only possible option."

"Great. Who, in their right mind – even a spirit – would consider that walking into a fire would be their only possible option? Maybe a Buddhist monk with a chip on his shoulder, but who else?"

"You ought to have more faith, Mr Rook. You shouldn't be so cynical, especially with *your* gifts."

"Gifts? You can call them gifts, but most of the time they're more like a burden."

"Mr Rook, magic teaches you one great truth. There's always a way, natural or supernatural. No matter what happens, there's *always* a way."

Jim looked at Laura with all her magical beads and her bangles and he wished that he could remember what it was like to be so innocent, and so enthusiastic, and to believe in the supernatural without any doubts. She was so pretty, so trusting in her grandmother's spells. Yes, there was always a way. But Jim knew from experience that the way through the world on the other side was dark, and as slithery and devious as a pit crowded with snakes and spiders, and that spirits and demons never honored their promises, any more than humans.

He laid his hand on her shoulder and said, "You're one of the best, Laura. One day, you're probably going to be the best witch in the whole of greater Los Angeles."

"You're going to go look for this spirit, aren't you?" asked Laura.

"Yes, I am."

"In that case, you'd better take this mirror with you. At least it'll give you a chance."

"I can't take this. It's a family heirloom."

"You have to. I haven't been a practising witch very long, Mr Rook, but if there's one thing I know, you can't fight what you can't see."

"She's right," put in Dottie, who was wearing a large strawberry-pink T-shirt with a transfer of George Clooney on the front, and voluminous white shorts. "I went to this party once, and they turned all of the lights off, and this guy really came on to me. I couldn't see him, but I wasn't going to fight him. That was my best night ever. Ever."

"That was your *only* night, ever," Laura put in, unkindly.

Dottie blushed, but Jim reached out and took hold of her hand and squeezed it. "If I were fifteen years younger," he said.

"I know," said Dottie. "If you were fifteen years younger, you wouldn't be any different from any of the guys who are fifteen years younger than you. Come on, Mr Rook, you're a great teacher, but I don't have any illusions."

Jim took the mirror from Laura. "I have illusions," he said. "But I'm going to hunt them down; and they won't threaten any of you, not any more."

Tibbles Two was acting out of character that evening. She sniffed at her food as if it were poisoned and then she went to sit on her chair on the balcony, staring northward, with the sinking sun shining orange in her eyes and the wind ruffling up her fur. Jim came out with a can of beer and leaned on the railing beside her.

"What's up, TT? Lost your appetite?"

The cat ignored him, and continued to stare toward the north.

"Something's bothering you, isn't it? Like to tell me what it is?"

Tibbles Two lifted her nose a little, but apart from that she gave him no indication at all of what she was thinking about.

"I have to leave you for a few days. You don't mind if your Uncle Mervyn takes care of you, do you? I won't be gone long. But there's some serious business that I have to attend to."

For the first time that evening, TT turned her head and stared at him. He had never seen an expression on any cat's face that was anything quite like it. Cats always looked condescending – and why not? They spend all their lives sleeping and dreaming and amusing themselves

158

while humans pander to their every whim as if they were minor royalty. But this expression was quite different. This was calculating and self-possessed, as if Tibbles Two had already made up her mind about something critical.

"Give me a sign, TT," said Jim. "A dancing Tarot card, anything."

TT continued to stare at him for a while. Then she jumped down from her seat and walked back inside. Jim hesitated for a moment and then followed her. She padded straight into his bedroom and bounded up onto the bureau, knocking over a bottle of Hugo Boss aftershave, and then on top of his closet, where he kept his airline bag. She sat on top of it and stared down at him imperiously.

"You're a cat. How do you know that I'm planning on taking a trip?"

TT yawned and licked her lips.

"Listen, you can't come with me. There's absolutely no way. Nobody takes a cat to the Arctic. Dogs, maybe, if they're working dogs. But did you ever see a sled pulled by a team of cats?"

TT stayed where she was, expressionless. In the end, there was nothing that Jim could do but shrug his shoulders and leave her. She was still there when he had finished his pizza, as watchful as the Snowman.

Late that evening, he drove around to the Hubbard house. Henry had already dragged all of his cold-weather gear from the closet, and it was heaped on the couch in the living-room: thick sweaters, fur-lined parkas, insulated boots – as well as rucksacks and harnesses and all kinds of assorted webbing belts and tackle that Jim couldn't even identify.

Jack was there, too, sprawled in an armchair, talking on the phone to one of his new college friends. "Yeah,

yeah. Just like I told him. You don't have to throw a hissy fit."

Jim saluted him and Jack saluted him back. Then he turned to Henry Hubbard. "I thought you ought to know that the Snowman was lurking around campus this evening. I actually saw it."

"You *saw* it? It's not supposed to be visible in temperatures over forty below."

"One of my students showed me a little magic trick with a mirror. I saw it all right, and it was just the way you described it."

Henry Hubbard looked at all of his equipment. He picked up a pair of snow-goggles with violet lenses and then dropped them back on to the couch. "I never thought I would wear any of this stuff again. I almost threw it all out."

"You're not going to chicken out on me, are you?"

Henry Hubbard glanced toward Jack, laughing as he talked to his friend. "No, Mr Rook. I'm not going to chicken out. There's too much at stake here, isn't there?"

He beckoned Jim through to the dining-room, where the table was covered in maps of northern Alaska. "I've taken the liberty of booking our flights to Fairbanks. We leave LAX at seven o'clock on Monday morning. We'll be staying overnight, and the following day we'll be flying by chartered plane up to Lost Hope Creek. I thought we'd try to reach Dead Man's Mansion from a different direction this time. We'll land on the south side of the Sheenjek glacier, here, instead of the north side. The terrain is much more difficult, but we'll have less than a third of the distance to cover. It's kind of a gamble, and it's a gamble we're probably going to lose if the weather sets in. But I calculated that with your lack of Arctic experience, you'd have more chance of survival if we went for a short, tough twenty-mile run, rather than an eighty-five-mile slog."

"Well, I should be pretty fit. I've been running up and down stairs at every opportunity. You know, to build up my stamina. My calf muscles are killing me."

"If anything will kill you, Mr Rook, it's the cold. It doesn't just bite at your fingers and your toes, it bites at your brain as well. It eats away your will to live."

"What about a snowmobile? You've arranged for a snowmobile?"

"The Sno-Cat will take us most of the way across the glacier. But when we reach the mountains on the other side, we'll have to go on foot. Seven or eight miles, at least."

Jim peered at the maps. "So where do you think Dead Man's Mansion actually is?"

"I can't say exactly. Last time we were relying on two so-called period maps and a whole lot of hearsay, but after my last experience I'm beginning to suspect that those maps may have been seriously misleading. In fact, they could well have been hoaxes – drawn by some imaginative trickster to persuade the University of Alaska to part with a large sum of money for a 'genuine historical document'."

"How about the hearsay?"

"I've read all the transcripts again and again. Most of them sound like the product of cabin fever or too much Yukon Jack whiskey; but there are two accounts which both describe the location of Dead Man's Mansion quite precisely. Look at this one. This was translated from the Inuit. 'The big house stands on a shelf of rock beside the Haunted Salmon glacier, which is a tributary of the Sheenjek. Behind it stands the crooked rock known as Death's Beckoning.' And this one, from a trapper called Jean-Pierre Troisrivières, who got lost in a blizzard in the same general area. 'Through the snow I saw a house

161

standing on a high rock. I had never seen such a house in the Arctic before. It was almost like a castle. Who built it and how it was built is a great mystery. To the right runs a glacier which the Esquimeaux call the Ghost Salmon Run, because it is supposed to carry the souls of every fish they kill slowly back out to sea, where they belong. Directly in line with its grand chimney stack is a rocky outcrop like a man's bent finger.'"

Henry Hubbard opened a file and took out a sheaf of satellite photographs which had been taken to assist in Amoco's oil exploration. "It's impossible to be one hundred per cent certain, but I believe that if Dead Man's Mansion exists, and if it's still standing, then it's *here*. You see the shadow that mountain is casting on the ice? Curved, like a beckoning finger. And you see the way the glacier kind of winds around this cliff? This topography fits both of those hearsay descriptions almost exactly."

Jim bent forward and examined the photograph with what he hoped was professional intensity. "Hmm . . . I don't see any house. I mean, with these satellites, you're supposed to be able to read the *National Enquirer* from five miles up in space, aren't you? And from all accounts, Dead Man's Mansion is a pretty sizeable joint."

"If it's half-buried in snow, and the sun isn't shining on it directly, then even a satellite wouldn't pick it up. The Air Force had the same problem looking for Soviet missile emplacements in Siberia."

"So how sure are you that this is the right spot? Seventy per cent sure? Sixty? Fifty-five and a half?"

"I don't know, Mr Rook. You can't calculate things like this mathematically. We may find out that Dead Man's Mansion is the same as the mountains of Crocker Land, nothing but a mirage."

"In which case?"

"In which case we have to start praying, Mr Rook. That's all we can do."

Jim looked at the map a little longer, and then he stood up and said, "By the way, my cat wants to come with us."

Twelve

Jim had a terror of flying in small airplanes. As they approached Lost Hope Creek, bumping and tilting against a south-west wind, he gripped his armrests so tightly that he almost dismantled his seat. All the same, he couldn't help being impressed by the scenery. They had flown for the past sixty miles over a dazzling river of ice, the Sheenjek Glacier; and the sky above them was so blue that it was almost black. On either side rose dark volcanic peaks, all of them hooded with snow, and in the distance Jim could see nothing but more mountains rising, peak after peak, as if all the mountains in the world had gathered here to greet them.

Henry Hubbard spent most of the flight talking to the pilot, a stringy man with a pecan-colored face and a restless toothpick in his mouth and no conversation. Jack sat hunched in his seat, staring out of the window. His relationship with his father was still strained, and once or twice, when Henry Hubbard had tried to remonstrate with him for slouching or sulking or talking back, he had said, "At least I didn't sell *your* soul!"

Every time he said it, Henry Hubbard physically winced, as if Jack had slapped his face. But he had kept his temper; and for his part, Jack had agreed to come along with them, to lend them his youth and his strength. As the shadow of their plane jumped and flickered across the jagged peaks and deeply riven crevasses that lay below them, Jim could see that they were going to need him.

The Cessna's engine made an alarming buzzsaw noise as they lost altitude and circled to the east to land at Lost Hope Creek. They passed over a settlement of five wooden houses with the Stars and Stripes flying over them, and circled again. Jim saw tiny figures emerging, and waving to them. The ground came up to meet them in a sudden rush, and they landed on skis on a short stretch of glassy ice that ran parallel to the glacier. The runway looked smooth from the air, but it was so bumpy that Jim thought that his teeth were all going to be rattled out of his head. Shifting his toothpick from right to left, the pilot swung them around to a halt only twenty feet before the runway deteriorated into stacks of dirty broken ice.

"Lost Hope?" he said, rhetorically, as he taxied them up toward the houses. "They don't even know the meaning of the word 'hope' in this dump, let alone what it's like to lose it." That was the longest sentence he had spoken all afternoon.

They climbed out of the airplane and Jim was immediately struck by the chill wind that was blowing off the glacier. After Los Angeles, Lost Hope Creek was so cold that it gave him a tight-bandana headache, just standing by the airplane waiting for the pilot to unload their bags for them.

The last piece of luggage out of the plane was a cardboard box with holes punched in it. The pilot handed it over to Jim and said, "You want to be careful with this. The dogs'll have it for lunch as soon as look at it."

"Thanks for the warning."

As they walked to the edge of the runway, they were greeted by two tall men in black parkas with furry hoods. One wore dark glasses through which an acute squint was faintly visible. The other sported a long greasy pigtail and hands that were covered in tattoos. There was even the tattoo of a snake's head emerging from his collar to lick at his right ear.

"Matty Krauss and Bill Wilderheim," said the man with the dark glasses. "Your supplies are all here. We've been having a little starting trouble with the Sno-Cat, but we should be able to get you moving for tomorrow morning."

They were joined by a short, slight Inuit in a sealskin coat. He reminded Jim of the Dalai Lama: bespectacled, courteous, and always smiling, although you could never discover at what. He gave each of them a soft, limp handshake.

"How do you do, gentlemen. My name is John Kudavak. I work for the state environmental protection agency."

"Keeping the ice nice, huh?" asked Jim.

"A little more than that, Mr Hubbard. I hope you won't mind if I come right to the point."

"He's Mr Hubbard. I'm Mr Rook."

John Kudavak turned to Henry Hubbard and said, "I'm sorry. But we're very concerned about this expedition of yours."

"What expedition? It's hardly an expedition. Just three of us taking a look-see, and filming some extra footage for my new documentary. How did you get to hear about it, anyhow?"

"I've been up here for a couple of weeks, seeing if we can set up a Sheenjek tourist center. Mr Krauss here told me what you had on your mind."

"So what's the objection?"

"Well, sir, we're always willing to encourage movie-makers who are keen to show the natural beauty of Alaska to a wider audience. But you're planning to look for Dead

Man's Mansion, so Mr Krauss tells me, and Dead Man's Mansion is not a designated site of natural beauty. As far as my office is concerned, it's a proscribed area. Quite apart from the fact that more than thirty people have died trying to find it in the past six years, which has put a severe strain on the state's rescue budget, the house is supposed to be built on a spot that it is very sacred to the Inuit people."

"Not the old Indian burial ground problem," said Jim.

John Kudavak gave him a thin, strained smile. "The place is sacred because it was here that the Great Immortal Being took out the eyes of his favorite angel, as a punishment for his jealousy, and charged him with taking care of those who are lost in the snow."

Jim turned to Henry Hubbard. "You didn't tell me that."

"Didn't I? Well, I don't think that it's particularly important."

"But that must have been why Edward Grace built it there in the first place. Don't tell me he put it there by accident."

"Mr Hubbard," put in John Kudavak, "I'm afraid that I'm going to have to pull the plug on this expedition. In my judgement, you're ill prepared and badly under-equipped; and I don't believe that what you're trying to do here is in the best interests of the local environment."

"This is crazy," said Henry Hubbard. "If we find Dead Man's Mansion, it could be the biggest tourist attraction in Alaska."

"These days, Mr Hubbard, there are many more ethnic Inuit people working for the environment agency. Like me, they believe in the story of the spirit who rescues people lost in the snow. Some of them have friends and relatives who claim to have been saved by the Snowman. The feeling in the agency these days is that they want the site to remain undiscovered. If it were found, it could constitute a threat to the integrity of their beliefs."

"Are we talking about a suggestion here, or a legal prohibition?"

"I have the authority to prevent you from undertaking an expedition to Dead Man's Mansion on the grounds that it would materially jeopardize the environment."

"We're taking one Sno-Cat across the glacier and the rest of the way we'll be traveling on foot. How can three pairs of feet materially jeopardize one of the harshest landscapes in the northern hemisphere?"

"Because if you find Dead Man's Mansion, your one Sno-Cat and three pairs of feet will be followed by hundreds of Sno-Cats and thousands more pairs of feet. You said yourself that it could become the biggest tourist attraction in Alaska."

"It's not just that, is it?" asked Henry Hubbard. "It's not just the landscape you're worried about."

"We're also concerned about the spiritual repercussions, yes."

"Spiritual repercussions? Why don't you speak English? You're worried that somebody's going to find this Snowman of yours, and stop it from doing what it always does when it rescues anybody."

"The Snowman is only a legend, Mr Hubbard, just like the angels in your own religion. But that is no excuse for anybody to compromise its sacred place. How would you feel if we Inuit trampled into your churches and denounced the Archangel Gabriel?"

"Bemused, to be frank."

"I'm afraid that doesn't change things. You will have to pack up all of your gear and return to Los Angeles."

Jim said, "Come on . . . I've sunk all my savings into this ill-prepared and badly under-equipped expedition."

"Then I am very sorry for you."

"We're still going to need paying for the Sno-Cat," put in Matty Krauss.

"You and your big mouth, you'll get your money," Henry Hubbard told him. Then – to John Kudavak, "Listen, supposing we sign a declaration that if we find Dead Man's Mansion, we will never reveal its location to anyone, will that satisfy you?"

"How do I know that you will honor such a declaration? Especially with the chance of making big money."

"Because I'm not doing this for the money. I'm not even doing it for glory. I'm doing it to save somebody's life. You're Inuit. You know what I'm talking about."

John Kudavak took off his wire-rimmed glasses. "Your Bible talks about an eye for an eye and a tooth for a tooth, doesn't it? That wasn't meant to encourage vengefulness, Mr Hubbard, although it seems that way today. In Biblical times, when somebody was wronged, he slaughtered the wrongdoer's entire family, right down to the last generation. Wiped out their name. All your Bible asks for is fairness. An eye for an eye, no more. A tooth for a tooth. And our belief is just the same."

"A soul for a soul," said Henry Hubbard, grimly.

John Kudavak replaced his glasses. "You will have to stay the night here, of course. But I expect you to arrange a flight back to Fairbanks by this time tomorrow."

They lodged that night in the house of a loopy old trader and his squat and silent Inuit wife. A big potbellied stove still stood in the center of the living-room, but it had dried flowers in it now, and all the heat came from butane fires. On the yellow-papered walls there were all kinds of unlikely pictures cut out of magazines and framed in home-made frames. Elvis Presley hung next to a view of the

Verrazano Narrows Bridge; and a hand-colored photograph of Rin-Tin-Tin hung next to the Leaning Tower of Pisa. The trader's name was William Crown and he had first come out to Alaska when he was twelve. He had been to Anchorage only once, to have an appendix operation, and he had been distinctly unimpressed. "Nobody never doing nothing for themselves in that place. What good is a man if he can't tie knots and he can't whittle and he can't gut a salmon? I've had seven wives and drunk half a bottle of whiskey every day and I can build you a kennel with one hand tied behind my back."

The squat and silent Inuit wife made them a meal of Sloppy Joes and spicy oven fries, and they sat in the overheated kitchen to eat it. So much for ethnic Inuit cooking, thought Jim. At least she hadn't served up jugged seagull. After huge platefuls of Rocky Road ice cream, they sat in the living-room while the squat and silent Inuit wife banged the saucepans in the sink like the climax of the *1812 Overture* and William Crown lit a cigarette.

"The doctor says I aint supposed to smoke, but I like to have one before I turn in. It aids restful sleep, which is a boon when the wind is shaking your roof at a hundut miles per hour and your woman is snoring and whooping and booming like a school of whales."

"You ever met anybody who's seen Dead Man's Mansion?" Henry Hubbard asked him.

"Some people say that they've seen it, but most of them are unreliable types; types you wouldn't trust to read a menu for you when you've sat on your glasses."

"I suppose you've never seen it."

"Nope, and I don't want to see it, neither. Because in my opinion it can't be seen, except for those who've looked death right slapbang in the face and I don't want to look death right slapbang in the face until it's my turn to go and take a look at him for good."

"What do you mean, it can't be seen?" Jim asked him.

"Exactly that. If your normal man went looking for it, he'd never find it, even if he walked right up to the door. But take a man who's nearly died, and he'll see it clear as any other house."

"Why do you think that?"

"You take the fellow who built it. Edward Grace, he looked death in the face, didn't he, when he nearly went down with the *Titanic*. And the story goes that he only employed builders who had been gold prospectors or miners or some such dangerous jobs – men who had cheated death. When it was finished they went home and talked about it, how grand it was. Everything super deluxe, by Alaska standards anyhow, like flush toilets and so forth.

"They weren't supposed to tell anybody where it was, but one of them was so pleased with his carpentry that he let it slip to his best friend that it was someplace close to the Ghost Salmon Glacier. This friend of his went to see it, but he searched all day and he couldn't find it anyplace. Others went, but they couldn't find it either. Only some kid saw it, some kid who'd nearly died of consumption, and he was so young and stupid that nobody believed him.

"To the ordinary eye, there was nothing there but rock, and ice. Not long after, the fellows that built it were laughed out of town because everybody thought they were doolally, pretending that they'd built a house, when there was no house there."

"That's why the environmental people can't find it," said Henry Hubbard. "And that's why the satellites can't pick it up. It doesn't exist in this world, only in the next."

"But you and I could see it," said Jim. "You've had a near-death experience, and so have I."

171

"We could see it if Mr Kudavak would allow us to go look for it."

"How can he stop us? There's only one of him and there's three of us."

"So what are you going to do, coldcock him? The environmental protection people have a whole lot of clout here in Alaska."

"I suppose they must. I mean, there's nothing much here *except* environment, is there? More environment than you could shake a stick at."

Henry Hubbard said, "We could take a risk. Get ready to leave at five o'clock in the morning, and head out of here before he can catch up with us."

Jim thought for a while, and then he said, "This guy armed, this Kudavak?"

"He'll have a rifle to protect himself against bears."

"All right, let's do it. After all, we don't exactly have a choice, do we? Either we find out how to beat this Snowman, or else the Snowman's going to catch Jack one day, and neither of us will be able to live with it, will we?"

"Jack?" asked Henry Hubbard.

But Jack was fast asleep in his chair, his head dropped back, his mouth wide open. With surprising tenderness, Henry Hubbard got up and covered him with his coat.

"Come on," said Jim. "We'd better hit the sack, too. Let's just hope that we can get that Sno-Cat running at five in the morning."

Jim didn't sleep that night. The sky never grew completely dark, and by three o'clock in the morning the sun was shining through the thin home-made drapes that covered his bedroom window. Tibbles Two didn't seem to have any trouble sleeping, however. She remained curled up at the foot of his bed, dead to the world, even when he made the blanket surge underneath her with his feet.

He wasn't entirely sure why he had brought her to Alaska with him. But in some indescribable way he felt safer when she was around. She seemed to know why he was here even more clearly than he did; and what he was supposed to do next. And there was no doubt in his mind at all that she was aware of the Snowman, aware of its presence, and aware of what it could do to them all.

At five after four he rolled out of bed and stiffly climbed into his clothes. Thermal long-johns, which made him feel like somebody's grandpappy; heavy-duty jeans; a red woollen shirt and a thick cable-knit sweater. He went to the kitchen and put on the coffee percolator, and then he stepped outside to look at the Arctic dawn.

The sky was the palest yellow, with tatters of high gray cloud, like a torn net-curtain. The sun was already gleaming over the snowcapped mountains off to the east. The wind was getting up: it made a feathery noise against his ears, and he could feel the thermometer dropping.

Henry Hubbard was out there already, walking around the battered old Sno-Cat. The Sno-Cat had a big squarish cabin made out of white-painted aluminum, insulated inside with metallic quilting. Instead of wheels it had four triangular caterpillar tracks at each corner. Henry Hubbard was checking the tracks for loose linkages and inspecting the hydraulic cables for leaks. He came over to Jim clapping his hands together to warm himself up.

"Beautiful morning," said Jim.

"Unh-hunh. Not for long. You feel that wind? There's something nasty coming from the north-west."

"I thought the summers up here were supposed to be pretty balmy."

"It depends. It's been a weird year for weather. El

Niño maybe. Maybe something else. Sunshine one minute, blizzards the next. Anyhow, since you're up, how about we grab ourselves a bite to eat and hit the trail? The further we can make it across the glacier before the weather breaks, the happier I'm going to be."

They sat in the kitchen and drank hot bitter coffee. William Crown's squat silent wife appeared and made them some heavy pancakes, which she drowned in maple syrup, and then left, slamming the door emphatically behind her. Jack came in looking frowzy with his hair sticking up and one shirt-tail hanging out. He sat down at the table and poured himself a large mug of coffee.

"Want a pancake?" asked Jim.

"I don't know. What are they like?"

"Hard to describe. Ever eaten a beret?"

By the time they had finished breakfast, Matty Krauss and Bill Wilderheim had appeared, carrying an assortment of spanners and wrenches. "You ready to roll? You want to start that engine and light out of here quick, before that Kudavak fellow hears what's going on, and starts off after you. Fussy little fellow, aint he? Never concerns himself with folk that have to make a living. Worries about animals, and trees, and all of that Inuit hocus-pocus."

Off to the west, the sky was darkening with alarming speed: a great bank of yellowish-gray snow-clouds climbed into the air like a massive volcanic eruption. The wind had risen to a thin, persistent sizzle, and it was filled with flying fragments of grit and ice. Jim and Jack and Henry Hubbard were all dressed up now in bright orange Arctic waterproofs, with hoods and snow-goggles and insulated gloves. Matty Krauss and Bill Wilderheim led them out to the Sno-Cat and opened the door for them. The perspex windows were milky and scratched and the cabin stank of diesel oil.

"She's pretty old," Matty Krauss told them. "We bought

her from some guy in the Yukon in 1976. He used her as a toolshed. He bought her from some guy in Alberta way back in 1968, and God alone knows where *he* got it from. But she runs okay, provided you treat her like the old lady she is."

He nodded at the cardboard box that Jim was carrying. "You aint seriously taking that moggie along, are you?"

Jim pressed his finger to his lips. "Don't upset her. She thinks *she's* taking *us.*"

They climbed into the Sno-Cat. There were four rudimentary seats made of aluminum piping and red leatherette, and stick controls for the two front steerable tracks. Henry Hubbard twisted the ignition key and the engine made a deep sluggish sound, like a hippopotamus turning over in its sleep. He twisted it again, and this time he managed to elicit a deep sluggish sound and two or three reluctant coughs. Jim leaned forward and said, "Try it again. My father used to have a diesel pickup, and it always took five turns to get it going in the winter."

Henry Hubbard tried again. More coughs, and a loud backfire, accompanied by two black smoke-signals from the exhaust pipe.

"They aint chosen a Pope yet," remarked Bill Wilderheim, laconically, as the black smoke drifted away.

Matty Krauss said, "Come on now, Mr Hubbard. That Kudavak fellow is only two cabins away. He's going to hear you starting up and he has the authority to stop you, you know that."

Henry Hubbard twisted the key again, and again. Each time the engine coughed and backfired and failed to start. At last, however, Bill Wilderheim climbed up the ladder and leaned into the cabin and twisted the key for him, and the engine burst into throbbing, rattling life.

"That's great," said Henry Hubbard. "How did you do that?"

Bill Wilderheim gave him a gappy grin and said, "I prayed, mister, that's what I did. I prayed and my prayer was answered."

"Well, I'll have to remember that, next time this heap fails to start."

"You do that, sir. You put your trust in the Lord."

Henry Hubbard released the brakes and the Sno-Cat began to grind its way along the ice-packed roadway that led to the Sheenjak Glacier. It wasn't fast: it could probably get up to thirty miles per hour in perfect weather conditions, on totally flat ice. In these conditions, their speedometer wavered between eight and fifteen.

Inside the Sno-Cat's cabin, the beating of the diesel engine and the clanking of the tracks was so loud that Jim had to shout at everybody. "Can't we go any faster?"

"We're doing top speed already! Any faster and we'll shake her to bits!"

Jim looked out of the Sno-Cat's rear window. Nobody appeared to be following them so far. They churned at a snail's pace down the steeply sloping gully that would take them on to the glacier, and inch by inch the five houses that made up the little community of Lost Hope Creek disappeared from view – all except for the Stars and Stripes, flapping over the trading post. In the summer, they never struck the flag at night because it never got dark.

"Looks like we've made it, Mr Rook," said Jack.

"Come on, Jack. You can call me Jim now. Save the 'mister' for English class."

They had little more than a hundred feet to go before they reached the brink of the Sheenjek Glacier, but Jim still kept a look-out behind them. They had made a hell of a noise starting up the Sno-Cat, and he didn't trust Matty

Krauss, either. If he alerted John Kudavak that they had gone, he would get his Sno-Cat back and get to keep his money, too.

"Hold on," called out Henry, revving the engine.

As he did so, however, Jim glimpsed headlights flashing through the milky, misted-up perspex. The headlights disappeared for two or three seconds, but then they suddenly reappeared, much nearer. Jim saw that they were being pursued by a green Ford Explorer, and the only person who had a green Ford Explorer in Lost Hope Creek was John Kudavak.

"It's Kudavak!" he shouted. "Step on it, Henry, he's gaining on us!"

"I'm flat out. This isn't a 'Vette, for Christ's sake!"

Jim glanced behind him again. The green Explorer was less than fifty feet away, its headlights jiggling as it negotiated the rough terrain. "Come on, Henry! He's going to catch us!"

The Ford was so close behind them now its front fender was almost touching the Sno-Cat's tracks. Kudavak tried to swerve around to the left-hand side and overtake them, but Henry Hubbard managed to steer the Sno-Cat so close to the side of the gully that Kudavak had to jam on his brakes and stop, or risk being jammed between the Sno-Cat's tracks and a wall of rock.

Kudavak tried overtaking them on the right-hand side. This time he managed to pull up alongside, and put down his window. They were close to the glacier now, less than 200 feet away, and the ground was so rough that his Explorer was bouncing up and down like a baby's pram.

"You have to stop!" he shouted at them. *"Dead Man's Mansion is a proscribed area! If you don't stop, I have the authority to call out the state police!"*

Jim slid back the Sno-Cat's window and yelled back,

"*We're taking a look, that's all! You can't stop us from taking a look!*"

"*What the hell do you mean you're taking a look? What the hell for?*"

Jim looked at Jack but all Jack could do was pull a face. Jim turned back to John Kudavak and shouted, "*No estoy en casa a Senor Fisgando!*"

At that instant, they reached the edge of the glacier. Even though the sky was rapidly darkening, it still shone dazzling white in the morning sun – a mile-wide river of ice that was gradually creeping its way through the Sad Horse mountains to the distant sea. The Sno-Cat climbed on to the choppy chunks of ice close to the shoreline, its engine growling, its triangular caterpillar tracks tilting, its cabin jolting from one side to the other. John Kudavak's Ford Explorer ran into a slope of broken ice chunks and almost toppled over before it came to a halt. John Kudavak climbed out and screamed at them in fury.

"You think that you can do anything you like! You think that you can pollute our seas and slaughter our wildlife and turn our people into drop-outs and drunks! You think that you can challenge our beliefs! But you can't! This is our land! This is ours!"

That was all that Jim could hear before the diesel engine drowned him out. The Sno-Cat reached some smoother terrain, and began to speed up, its tracks leaving a fine spray of ice behind it.

Henry Hubbard leaned back and said, "If we can keep this up, we should reach Dead Man's Mansion by midday tomorrow."

"Provided it exists."

"It exists, Jim. I know it exists. The closer I get, the surer I am."

There was a lengthy silence between them as the Sno-Cat

ground its way across the glacier. They were bumped and buffeted against the sides of the cabin, but they were dressed in so many layers of clothes that they barely felt it. TT began to mewl inside her box, so Jim let her out and sat her on his lap, so that she could look out of the misted-up window. She didn't seem to want any food or drink. She sat upright staring northward, her ears folded back, and Jim had the strangest feeling that she was coming home.

After a long while, Jack sat up and touched his father's shoulder. "Dad . . . I just want to tell you that what you're doing here . . . well, I really appreciate it."

"I'm doing what I have to do, that's all."

"No, you're not. I know you didn't mean to trade my soul. I know you must have thought that the Snowman was some kind of hallucination. I would have thought it was, too."

"I still shouldn't have done it."

"It doesn't matter any more. I know you never wanted to come back here. I know what that thing did to you – taking your pride and your courage and everything. But it takes much more courage to come back when you're scared than it does when you're not, doesn't it? And who needs to be proud when other people are proud of them?"

Henry Hubbard looked quickly at Jim and Jim could see that there was a tear glistening in his right eye.

Jack said, "I'm trying to make you understand that I forgive you for what you did. Whatever happens here . . . even if we can't find Dead Man's Mansion. I know that you never really meant to hurt me."

Henry Hubbard gripped his son's hand and said, "Thanks, Jack," in a soft, husky voice. After that, they traveled in silence again for a while. The dark clouds began to mount the sky from the west, and a fine snow began to blow horizontally across the glacier, like thistledown. The sun was still shining, but Jim reckoned that it would soon be overwhelmed. He hoped to God that they could cross the exposed surface of the glacier before a blizzard caught up with them.

"By the way," said Jack, "what was that you said to John Kudavak back there? Was that Spanish?"

"*No estoy en casa a Senor Fisgando.* It means keep your schnozzle out of my business. Strictly translated, 'I'm not at home to Mister Snoopy'."

Within an hour, the clouds had completely swallowed the sky, and it was so dark that Henry had to switch on the bank of spotlights on top of the Sno-Cat's roof. The wind blew harder and harder, until it rocked the Sno-Cat's cabin and screamed between the tracks like a ghost train. The snow was still quite light, however, whirling in the spotlights and pattering against the windows.

Henry turned around and shouted, "We're almost halfway across! So long as the snow holds off, we should make it okay!"

Jim strained his eyes and peered at the gloomy landscape ahead. Through the flying snow, he thought he could make out a jagged shadow crossing the ice at a sharp diagonal, only thirty or forty feet in front of them.

"Henry! What's that ahead of us?"

Henry turned his head and immediately brought the Sno-Cat to a shuddering halt. The jagged shadow was a deep crevasse – wide enough for the Sno-Cat to have tipped into. They climbed down from the cabin into the wind, and walked over to the edge. The crevasse was not only wide, it was so deep that they couldn't see how far it went down.

"What do we now?" said Jim.

"We can't cross over, so we'll just have to follow it as

far as it goes. It looks like it's going to take us way off course."

"Better get going, then. Let's hope that it doesn't stretch across the whole damn glacier."

They heaved themselves back into the Sno-Cat and Henry started it up. He steered it along the left-hand side of the crevasse, making sure that he kept the tracks well away from the brink. "I saw the edge of a crevasse give way once, with two men and a sled and a dog-team standing on it. They went down so deep that they broke every bone in their bodies, dogs and men both, and they were frozen to death before we could winch them out."

Henry kept on talking, but he couldn't relax his concentration for a second, because the crevasse zig-zagged so unpredictably. It also took them further and further to the west, more than a mile from the place where they had planned to reach the opposite bank.

They were more than two thirds of the way across when Jack lifted his woolly hat clear of his ear and said, "What's that? Can you hear something?"

Jim listened but all he could hear was the thrumming of the engine. But Jack said, "There it is again. It's coming closer, whatever it is."

Jim strained his ears, and this time he *could* hear something. It was a *flacker-flacker-flacker* noise, the same kind of noise that he used to make when he was a kid, by clothes-pinning a stiff square of cardboard on to his bicycle wheel.

"Engine's not giving up on us, is it, Henry?" he shouted. "Sounds like a bearing's gone."

"Don't think so," Henry replied. "Oil pressure's up, heat's steady."

Still the *flacker-flacker-flacker* grew louder. It sounded as if it were coming from the south-west, close behind them.

Jim peered out of the Sno-Cat's window but he couldn't see anything other than whirling snow and clouds the color of rotten cauliflower.

Jack said, "Jim, that sounds like a—"

And it was then that a white Alouette helicopter suddenly appeared in front of them, dipping and dancing in the wind. It switched on a blinding searchlight that shone directly into the Sno-Cat's cabin, and a hugely amplified voice announced, *"Stop! Alaska State Police! You are approaching a prohibited area! Turn back immediately!"*

The helicopter circled around them, so that they could see the Alaska State Police insignia, and they could see the goggled trooper sitting at the open door, with a high-powered rifle resting across his legs.

"Turn back immediately! We will escort you back to Lost Hope Creek!"

"What are you going to do?" asked Jim. "We can't turn back now – not after coming this far."

"Then we'll carry on," said Henry. He revved up the engine again, and the Sno-Cat continued to crawl forward across the glacier, with the State Police helicopter pirouetting all around it.

"Turn back immediately! Turn back immediately!"

Henry's response was to press the accelerator even harder, so that the Sno-Cat picked up speed to eighteen miles per hour.

"Turn back immediately, or we will open fire to disable your vehicle!"

"Do you hear that?" said Henry. "They're going to start shooting at us. Typical police response to anything they don't understand."

He kept on driving steadily forward, while the helicopter's searchlight shone through the cabin so brightly that none of them could see.

182

Jim said, "Keep going. With any luck they won't have the nerve to open fire. This is Alaska, after all. Not LA."

They picked up speed as they roared down a steep, slanting incline, the ice crackling and creaking underneath their tracks. Close beside them, the helicopter reared and side-stepped like a skittish horse.

"What did I tell you?" said Jim. "Hayseeds in furry hats. They won't hurt us."

At that moment they heard an explosive bang and the Sno-Cat's engine let out a wounded scream. Another bang, and another, and a bullet punched right through the roof of the Sno-Cat's cabin and blew a hole through TT's cardboard box. TT, sitting on her own by the window, didn't even jump. Her attention was still fixed on the north, her ears sloped back, her eyes slitted, and all the time she was softly purring – a purr that you could hear only if you sat right next to her.

The helicopter circled around behind them. Jim heard another shot, and then another, and the moaning sound of ricochets. They were shooting at the track assemblies now, trying to damage the tracks or pierce the hydraulic hoses. Another bullet struck the cabin roof, flying off into the snow; and yet another punctured the windshield.

"They're going to kill us," said Jim. "Forget what I said about hayseeds in furry hats. These guys mean business."

"So what do we do?" Henry demanded. "Stop? Give up? And sacrifice Jack to the Snowman?"

"Can we get to Dead Man's Mansion on foot?"

"From here? It must be seventeen or eighteen miles."

"But can we do it?"

"Like I told you, it's very difficult terrain. It depends on the weather. It depends on how determined we are."

"But can we do it?"

183

"I guess we have a seventy per cent chance. With a little help from the Great Immortal Being."

"Then here's what we're going to do. Jack and I will jump out of the Sno-Cat when the helicopter's light is pointing the other way, and we'll hide ourselves in the snow. You turn the Sno-Cat toward the crevasse and leave the gas pedal jammed down with that fire-extinguisher. Then you jump out, and hide yourself, too."

"You're crazy."

"Do you have any better suggestions? Either we stop, and they arrest us, and take us back to Fairbanks; or else we don't stop, and they shoot us; or else we try to get away."

Henry hesitated for a moment, but then the helicopter came roaring closer, and three more high-powered bullets penetrated the engine compartment. Steam began to hiss from the hood, and the oil-pressure gauge swung dramatically downward.

"Henry – we don't have any alternative. Not if we're going to save Jack."

"Okay," said Henry. "Let's do it. Jack – you take that rucksack with all the supplies. Jim – you carry the tent. What are you going to do with your cat?"

"TT can ride inside my coat. I don't think any other cat would do it, but TT seems to be more determined to get to Dead Man's Mansion than we do."

Again they were blinded by bright blue halogen light. The helicopter marksman fired three more shots – one of which banged through the Sno-Cat's cabin with a noise like somebody stamping on a tin roof.

"That's enough for me," said Jim. "Let's get out of here."

As the helicopter swung away, he opened the Sno-Cat's door and climbed out onto the ladder. The wind was screaming even more loudly now, so loudly that the noise of the helicopter was almost drowned out. Jack picked up a limp, unprotesting TT and handed her down. TT's fur blurted in the wind, and she turned her face away, but she didn't struggle. Jim hesitated for a moment, and then he dropped on to the ice. He stumbled and almost fell, but he managed to catch his balance and jog off sideways into the darkness, with TT dangling under his arm. It didn't take him long to find an icy outcrop and drop down underneath it, covering his orange survival outfit with powdered snow. Jack jumped out next, rolling over and over with his backpack. He picked himself up and looked all around him, bewildered, but Jim gave him his taxi-hailing whistle and he came running over to join him.

The Sno-Cat trundled on, heading toward the crevasse. The helicopter swooped around it yet again, firing three more shots. But it didn't slow down. Henry must have wedged the fire-extinguisher on top of the gas pedal by now, and it would be only seconds before he jumped out, too.

Just here, the crevasse was more than forty feet wide and it ran straight across the Sno-Cat's slowly grinding path. It was impossible to tell how deep it was, but a crevasse as wide as that could reach down right to the underbelly of the glacier, where the unimaginable tonnage of ice above it melted the Sheenjek river into water.

"*Time to abandon ship, Henry,*" urged Jim, under his breath.

But the Sno-Cat roared onward, pouring out thick black smoke and high-pressure steam, and still Henry didn't jump out.

"Come on, Dad," said Jack, desperately.

185

"It's okay," Jim told him. "Your dad's cutting it a little fine, that's all."

The Sno-Cat kept on going. Its engine was on fire now. They could see the bright orange flames licking out of the engine vents. It was less than ten feet from the edge of the crevasse, but even though the door was swinging open, there was still no sign of Henry Hubbard.

"Dad," said Jack. It sounded like a prayer.

The Sno-Cat's engine suddenly flared up; and the helicopter swung around and picked it out with its searchlight. It was only then that Jim saw the dark figure lying at an awkward angle over the control sticks, and the spray of red blood and yellow brains up against the perspex window. One of the last three shots must have penetrated the Sno-Cat's cabin and hit Henry in the head.

Before the Sno-Cat reached the very edge of the crevasse, the ice began to collapse under its weight. Abruptly, it tilted sideways, its tracks racing, its engine flaring up. The last that Jim saw of Henry Hubbard was a silhouette of a man being flung to one side like a marionette, one arm raised in a jerky, involuntary farewell. Then, with an ear-splitting crack of ice, and a tortured scream of metal and machinery, the Sno-Cat dropped into the crevasse, and disappeared.

There was a long moment of tumbling and banging as it collided with one side of the crevasse, and then the other. The helicopter came dipping down to see what had happened, shining its seachlight right down into the depths.

Jack shouted, *"You bastards! You bastards! You killed my dad!"* He tried to scramble on to his feet but Jim snatched the strap of his rucksack and dragged him back.

"They killed him, and they're going to pay for it. But if you let them see you now, this whole expedition is finished."

"They shot him! They shot him! He was my dad and they shot him!"

"They'll pay, I promise you! You and I were witnesses. They'll pay."

At that instant, there was a deafening explosion, and a thunderous ball of orange flame rolled out of the crevasse. The helicopter tilted away, but the huge upsurge of heat must have caught it off-balance, because it suddenly keeled over, and the tips of its rotor-blades bit into the ice.

It happened so fast that that Jim could hardly follow what was happening. The helicopter's rotors burst into thousands of flying fragments, which whistled all around them like boomerangs. Its fuselage dropped on its side and hit the ice, but then it bounced off and toppled into the crevasse, following the Sno-Cat. There was a sharp series of crackles and cracks, and then a soft, emphatic *whoommfff!* Another ball of fire rolled up into the air, followed by a rolling column of acrid smoke.

With their hands lifted to protect their faces, Jim and Jack approached the crevasse and peered over the edge. Sixty feet below, fires raged like a medieval vision of hell. The heat was so intense that the ice on either side was melting in bubbling cascades and then boiling. Tangled together in a last destructive embrace, the helicopter and the Sno-Cat were both fiercely burning, and the crevasse was criss-crossed with ladders of wreckage. Jim saw the helicopter pilot still sitting in his seat, as if he were sitting on a high blazing throne, his head thrown back, his uniform charred black and fire pouring out of his open mouth.

Jim took hold of Jack's arm and led him away. Jack's eyes streamed with tears, but then Jim's were streaming, too, from the heat and the smoke.

They sat down for a while, exhausted, shocked, saying nothing, while showers of sparks flew out of the crevasse and danced amongst the snowflakes. Then Jim stood up and said, "Time to go on, Jack. They'll be sending more helicopters soon. We can cry about this later."

Thirteen

With each hour that passed, the blizzard grew fiercer. It was so dark that it could have been two o'clock in the morning instead of two o'clock in the afternoon. The wind screamed at them from the north-west, all the way across the Bering Straits from Siberia. Jim opened his stormproof coat and tucked Tibbles Two into his sweater. She didn't struggle, even when he tugged the zipper right up over her ears.

Side by side, keeping so close together that they kept jostling each other, Jim and Jack plodded along the edge of the Sheenjek crevasse. Jim had seen the blizzards that Henry Hubbard had faced on his videotapes of his last expedition, but he had never appreciated how strong the wind was, and how stinging the snow, and to what agonizing degrees the temperature could drop. Although it was summer, it was probably forty-five below, but the windchill factor made it seem half as cold again. In spite of his hood and his gloves and all of his layers of clothing, Jim felt as if every last calorie of heat had been leached out of his bones, and that he would never again know what it was like to be warm.

The snow became furious. Jim and Jack clung close together. One of them would have to stray only five or six paces and he would disappear into all of that madly whirling whiteness, and be impossible to find. And the blizzard never relented: it went on and on, until Jim felt as

189

if he were being forced to stare at a blank television screen for hours on end. All that gave him any sense of direction was the edge of the crevasse, which he knew was taking them further and further west of the place they had been aiming for; and his compass, whose dial frosted over every time he brought it out to look at it; and Tibbles Two. Every time he unzipped his jacket to make sure that she hadn't suffocated, her eyes were staring fixedly northward.

They reached the edge of the glacier shortly before sunset – although they couldn't have known for sure, because they hadn't seen the sun for hours. The wind was so strong now that they had to walk with their backs bent. They were both exhausted and Jim began to wonder if it was less of a risk to turn back to Lost Hope Creek. There had to be another way of fighting the Snowman, apart from trudging for miles and miles through sub-zero temperatures, looking for a mansion that was said to be nothing more than a mirage.

He patted Jack on the shoulder and they crouched down together behind a low curve of rocks. "Let's take a rest," he said. "We still have another ten miles to go, at least."

Jack took off his snow-goggles. "You don't think he suffered, do you?"

"Your dad? No way. He wouldn't have known what hit him."

"I don't know whether he was a coward or a hero or just plain stupid."

Jim didn't say anything. He was too cold to think of anything witty and uplifting; and, in any case, Jack would have to make up his own mind, as time went by, about his father's last expedition and his tragic death.

He took a Snickers bar out of his pocket and snapped it, handing half of it to Jack. "Watch your teeth. In this climate, it's like taking a bite out of a crowbar."

Jack said, "Forget it. I don't want anything to eat."

"I know how you feel, but force yourself. If we're going to make it to Dead Man's Mansion, you're going to need the sugar."

"Do you think it's worth it?"

"What, carrying on? It's not going to be easy, but what else are we going to do?"

"Turn back, maybe? Give it all up? My dad's dead, what does the Snowman want with *me* any more?"

"Believe me, it wants you."

"And what about you? Why should you be risking your life? We've lost all of our navigation equipment and we don't even have enough supplies, do we?"

"Stop being so pessimistic. I've got twenty-three bars of rock-hard Snickers."

"And what else? A cat, and a mirror that Laura Killmeyer gave you? How are we going to survive with *those*?"

The wind roared around the curve in the rocks like a living beast, and snow flew into their faces in a blinding frenzy. They were sitting only two feet away from each other, yet they could scarcely see each other. Jim said, "You can go on, or you can quit, it's up to you. Personally, my survival instinct tells me to quit. But then I think about Ray and Suzie and I think about you . . . what's going to happen to you if we don't find out how to get this Snowman off your back. And I think about your father. He made a mistake, but he gave up everything to put it right."

Jack brushed the snow off his face. "I don't know. All my life, I've always seemed to be doing things because of *him*. Like living in Alaska, because he had such an obsession with the Arctic, and the Inuit. I'm half Inuit, but that doesn't mean I want to live in some dogsled community eating fish and frozen caribou for the rest of my life. Coming to California – coming to West Grove College – that was the first time I ever felt independent, the first time I ever felt free. And what did I find out? I couldn't be free, because my father had sold my soul."

"That sounds to me like a vote to carry on."

"I don't have any alternative. You know that."

They climbed to their feet. Jim knotted a length of orange cord to his belt and tied the other end to Jack's rucksack. That way, even if they lost sight of each other, they wouldn't become separated. They began to trudge slowly eastward, making their way to the point where the Sno-Cat was supposed to have reached the far side of the glacier.

Jim gave Jack a thumbs-up sign. Then he bowed his head and carried on with the wearisome business of walking.

He thought about a whole jumble of things as he walked. He thought about Peary and Amundsen and Scott, and all the other men who had risked their lives to conquer the world's coldest places. He wondered what it was that had given them the strength and the character to carry on. The cold itself induced a kind of madness. It was like being seriously drunk. Your brain had the confidence but your body didn't have the co-ordination. And the flying snow was almost intolerable. It confused all sense of direction and distance. One second it was blowing to the right; then to the left; then it was swirling in circles.

They must have been walking for over three hours when Jim called a temporary halt for another Snickers bar and a check on their position. He took out his compass but his hands were so numb that he dropped it into snow. He bent down, furiously raking at the snow with his gloves, but there was no sign of it anywhere. He took one glove off, and carried on frantically searching, but Jack said, "Forget it, Jim. It's gone. And put your glove back on. You don't want to lose your fingers."

"I don't even know which direction we're supposed to be headed."

"It's north, isn't it, Dead Man's Mansion?"

"Sure. North. But at what longitude? In this weather, we could pass within a couple of hundred feet and not even know that it was there. Maybe Tibbles can help."

Jim pulled down his zipper. Tibbles Two was still there; but she was sleeping; and even when Jim shook her violently up and down she refused to respond.

"She's bluffing," he said. He took off his glove and pulled back one of her eyelids, revealing a staring green eye, but she immediately closed it again, and carried on purring.

They stood beneath a black sky, lost in a never-ending torrent of snow. Jim reckoned that they must be very close to the place where the Ghost Salmon Glacier joined up with the Sheenjek; and where the rocks rose up on the west side of the glacier valley, their black faces scoured by centuries of fierce weather and gradually inching ice. But he wasn't totally sure. The Ghost Salmon Glacier curved right around before it joined the Sheenjek, and he didn't know whether he was looking west or east; or even north, where Dead Man's Mansion stood.

But now TT began to mewl and scratch and to struggle restlessly inside his windcheater. In the end, she stuck her claws right through his woolly cable-knit sweater and into his chest.

"Jesus!" he exclaimed, ripping down the zip-fastener and allowing TT to tumble out onto the snow. She landed on her feet, vigorously shook herself, and paused to sniff at the snow. Then she bounded off to stand on a small rocky outcrop only thirty or forty feet away. She was almost lost in the whirl of snowflakes. Sometimes she was plainly in view; at other times she vanished completely, as if she had never existed. But at last Jim saw her right on the very peak of the rock, and she was staring ahead of her, unwavering, unflinching, even though she couldn't have been able to see more than either of them.

"Come on," urged Jim. "She knows where it is; and she's getting excited; so it can't be too far to go now."

"We've lost our geo-sat positioning equipment so we're trusting a *cat*?"

"Do you have any better suggestions?"

"As a matter of fact, maybe," said Jack. He pointed to a sloping bank of ice off to the left of the outcrop where Tibbles Two was sitting. Jim peered at it and said, "I don't know what the hell you're talking about."

But even as he was speaking, he thought he glimpsed the shudder of long white robes in the darkness; and a tall shapeless hood; and a bony hand carrying a staff. The apparition melted away, almost as soon as he saw what it was. But Jim was furious with tiredness and despair. He had no energy left for riddles or mysteries or optical illusions. He picked up his rucksack and said, "Let's go. We've found ourselves a guide now. We've found ourselves a fourth man."

Jack looked wildly in every direction. "It's here, isn't it? You've seen it."

Jim grasped his arm and said, "Trust me, Jack, for God's sake. This is destiny. This is one of those times when you find yourself doing exactly what the Tarot cards predicted, no matter how hard you've been trying to do something else."

"But it wants my *soul*, Jim. Not just my body, that would be bad enough. My *soul*, man. *Me*. Everything that makes me who I am. And I wouldn't die."

Staring at Jack through the teeming snow, Jim suddenly began to understand who he was – the 'who' that he was so frightened not to lose. When he had first arrived in Special Class II, he had appeared to be cool and self-possessed, even arrogant. But he had the same contradictory mixture of adventurousness and self-doubt that his father had shown; and he had something else, something very special: a deep belief in the mystic world that must have come from his Inuit mother.

"Remember one thing," said Jim. "The Snowman is duty bound to guide us, and save our lives. That's its job description. The setting-up comes later."

The tall white figure was still standing in the blizzard, less than fifty feet away. It looked even taller and even stranger than the image that Jim had seen in the mirror, standing in the woods at West Grove. Maybe the snow was distorting it. Maybe he was seeing it face-to-face for the very first time, unreflected, unshrunken. But it terrified him. It was his nemesis, without a face. And what made it even more frightening was the fact that he had to rely on it, to save himself.

He grasped Jack's arm and said, "Come on, Jack. We can do this. You're young and I'm crazy. What better qualifications do we need?"

The tall figure moved off into the blizzard. Jim and Jack began to follow it, climbing the slope until they reached the place where Tibbles Two was still standing, her fur thick with snowflakes. Jim knelt down and she jumped toward him. He picked her up and stowed her into the front of his coat, where she wriggled and squirmed until she could make herself comfortable.

They found themselves climbing knee-deep in snow up a steep, angled gradient. It was snowing so hard that visibility was reduced to less than twenty feet, but the terrain reminded Jim of the maps that Henry Hubbard had shown him in Los Angeles, and he guessed that they were gradually climbing up the left bank of the Ghost Salmon Glacier. Within five or six miles they should reach Dead Man's Mansion – always supposing that it existed, and that it wasn't simply a deception.

Several times the blizzard was so blinding that Jim and Jack couldn't work out where they were going. But whenever they stopped, clearing their goggles and staring around them, the tall white figure was always there, off to their left, waiting for them, waiting to guide them on.

For Jim, most of the journey up the side of the glacier was a disconnected blur, like a broken film whipping through a cine-projector. His feet were so cold that he could no longer feel them. His fingertips burned with frostbite. Every breath dropped down into his lungs like two bucketfuls of chilly cement. He couldn't see, he couldn't hear anything; he couldn't even think.

Several times he slipped and dropped to his knees. But whenever he knelt in the snow, the tall figure in the white robes was always waiting for him, scarcely visible, and he knew that it was going to guide him to safety.

"I'm coming, damn you," he croaked, and climbed up on to his feet again, and carried on. And only a few feet behind him, connected by his orange cord, came Jack, staggering with every step, his head thrown back in tiredness and delirium, but still walking – still managing, somehow, to drop one foot in front of the other.

Jim lost count of time. In any case the dial of his watch was frozen over with a solid pebble of ice. The ground grew steeper and steeper, until they had to climb it on their hands and knees. The tall figure stayed well ahead of them, on their left, occasionally turning as if to make sure that they were following it, but most of the time striding ahead with its tall stick penetrating the snow, its head slightly bent, oblivious to their suffering.

They climbed higher and higher. Jim reckoned they must have scaled a slope of more than 500 feet. He was well beyond gasping. Every muscle in his body felt as if it had been taken out and beaten with a steak mallet. Behind him, Jack was groaning with pain, but he managed somehow to keep on climbing.

And then, the ground began to level off. The snow began to spin away, and dance in diminishing eddies, and the clouds began to clear, as if somebody were tearing them apart by hand.

And then, as they were able to stand up straight, they saw that they were standing on a high rocky shelf, above the snowclouds, with the moon shining pale and true, and the turmoil of the blizzard well below them. There were stars scattered everywhere, ridiculous showers of stars, and mountain-peaks glistening for fifty or sixty miles in every direction.

But the figure beckoned them on, more urgently now, up a gradual rise; and as they reached the top of it they saw what had always been drawing them here.

It was a huge Gothic house, built in the style favored by wealthy self-made men just before the First World War. It stood overlooking a valley that was now filled with clouds, but which must have afforded it extraordinary views, all across Ghost Salmon Glacier and the mountain ranges through which the glacier crept its way, carrying the thousands of souls of the Inuit's dead catches.

The house had a balcony overlooking the valley, and a veranda all around, and two high chimney-stacks. Except for the chimney-stacks, which were constructed of granite, it was built of solid gray seasoned timber, which must have been cut from the forests further down the valley, and dragged up here by teams of dogs, since the weather was far too severe for horses.

The house was embellished with decorative balconies and carved shutters and circular windows high up in the roof. It was ghostly and derelict and silvery-gray in the light of the moon, the haunted house to end all haunted houses; and yet it had a period magnificence all of its own, a ruined grandeur, just like the *Titanic* at the bottom of the ocean.

"Dead Man's Mansion," said Jack, with awe.

"And it's not an illusion; or a mirage; it's real."

"It's real to us. But maybe there are some people who can never see it."

"It's real, for God's sake," said Jim. He walked across the last stretch of icy ground and walked up the steps onto the verandah. "It's real. Dead Man's Mansion. It actually exists."

The tall figure watched them from a distance, half-hidden in the darkness. Jim said to Jack, "You wait. It won't go away. It's going to want something for bringing us here. And it's probably going to want your soul, too."

They walked along the veranda until they reached the front door. It was then that Tibbles Two began to struggle and thrash inside Jim's coat. She fought so hard to get out that he had to untie the laces around his waist and let her drop out downward on to the wooden boards. Immediately she rushed toward the front door, which was slightly ajar, and pushed it open.

Jim approached the front door with less enthusiasm. It was huge and heavy and cracked by the weather. A huge bronze knocker hung in the middle of it, cast in the shape of a snarling wolf. Jack approached it and took off his glove, and touched it very cautiously, right on the nose.

"The Wolf-Spirit. The evil one who chases Inuit hunters

and kills them when their dogs are lame or their sleds get trapped in the ice."

"So what's it doing on this door?"

"It's there to keep away lesser mischievous spirits. It's there to show that the person who lives in this house has considerable powers; and is not to be monkeyed with."

Jim hesitated for a moment before opening the front door any further. The tall figure was still watching them, standing close to a rocky outcropping that looked just like a huge beckoning figure. But it made no approach and it gave them no sign. Maybe it hadn't yet completed its task of saving their lives: they were still miles away from safety, in a freezing and hostile environment, with no way of calling for help. The way the legend went, it had to save a life before it could exact a payment for it.

"Well, let's take a look and see if the stories are all true," said Jim, pushing open the front door. They stepped inside and found themselves in a large hallway with paneled walls and a brown and white tiled floor. An Edwardian hat-stand stood by the door, on which a frozen Derby hat still hung beside a half-rotted fur *chapka*. There was a large mirror opposite, with a gilded frame. It was misted by age and cold, and its mercury backing had become veined with black, but they could still make out their own fearful images in it, as if they were trespassing on somebody else's long-vanished life.

Jim nudged open a door to the right. It swung open with eerie ease, revealing a drawing-room crowded with heavy, frozen furniture. A crystal chandelier hung from the ceiling, its original glass pendants covered by sparkling stalactites. Everything had the whiteness of intense cold: the same whiteness of George Mallory's skin, when they had discovered his body on Everest. Everything looked as if it had been breathed on by cold and death and passing time.

They left the drawing-room and walked across to the dining-room. The door was open a little way, and Jim suspected that this was where they would find Tibbles Two. He opened it up, and saw by the powdery moonlight that illuminated the room almost as bright as day that he was right. Tibbles Two was sitting on a chair beside the large oak dining-table, her head proudly raised, her eyes slitted in complete satisfaction. Somehow, in some extraordinary way, Tibbles Two had come home.

More than that, she had found her master. Because sitting in a carver chair at the far end of the dining-table, almost perfectly preserved by the cold, was the bleached-faced figure of a man in a long black overcoat, his hair white and tufty but still mostly intact, his eye-sockets blackened and crinkly like prunes, his nostrils gaping, his lips drawn back over higgledy-piggledy teeth that were startlingly yellow. Underneath his overcoat he still wore a three-piece suit, a starched collar and a bow-tie. His right hand lay on the table in front of him, still clutching a pen, and there were sheets of paper scattered everywhere, as well as Tarot cards and other fortune-telling cards of every description. Jim recognized the nine of spades from Grimaud's *Sybille des Salons*: the death card, hollow-eyed, carrying a scythe.

"So here he is," said Jim. "Edward Grace, in person."

He walked around the dining-table. His breath fumed with every step. The temperature must have been sixty degrees below, and even in high summer it must have always been well below freezing. Edward Grace had been preserved almost as well as a body in a cryogenic center, waiting for the day when medical science could find a way to revive him.

Jim lifted his rucksack off his back, lowering it carefully on to the floor, because he was still carrying Laura's mirror. He approached Edward Grace's body while Jack hung back a little way, looking around at the frozen velvet drapes and the frozen ornaments and the shelves stacked with solid-frozen books.

Underneath Edward Grace's left hand lay a leather-bound notebook. Jim tried to ease it out from underneath his fingers but they all appeared to be fused together by the intense cold, in the same way that Ray Krueger's fingers had been fused to the railing. He tried again, tugging it harder this time, but it still refused to budge. He made sure that Jack wasn't looking, and he hit Edward Grace's fingers with a karate chop, snapping his frozen fingers off at the knuckles. The notebook came free, even if it did have three white fingers still attached to the front cover.

He tried to pry the notebook open, but the pages were stuck together, as inseparable as the slices of a deep-frozen loaf. Turning to Jack, he said, "Light us a fire, will you? If we're going to survive the night, we're going to need some heat."

"What with?"

"You have a cigarette-lighter, don't you? Break up some of this furniture and burn it."

"But it must be priceless, some of it."

"No, it's not. It's ugly, heavy, 1900s mahogany. The stuff that Sears, Roebuck used to sell to Nebraska farmers with delusions of grandeur."

"Okay, if you say so."

They broke up several chairs by kicking them and smashing them against the floor. Up here in Dead Man's Mansion, miles from any civilization, the noise seemed twenty times louder than normal, and they had to stop now and again to listen to the silence. Jack piled chair-legs into the grate and soon got them crackling and spitting. Jim propped the notebook next to them, hoping that it wouldn't take long to thaw. It was only three or four minutes before the fingertips dropped off the cover into the grate, and Jim was able to scoop them up with the ash-shovel and drop them discreetly into the blaze.

"This guy was supposed to have found the secret of destroying the Snowman, wasn't he?" asked Jack. "I mean, this is the whole reason we're here, right? So where's the secret?"

The dining-room was filled with dancing, jumping light from the hearth. The shadows on the walls looked like hopping Inuit wonder-workers in their mukluks. The air began to feel distinctly warmer, and as it did so, all kinds of smells began to emerge – smells that had been locked inside this frozen mausoleum of a house for over three quarters of a century. The smell of Berlinwork rugs, and quarter-sawed oak, and horsehair upholstery. Smells that existed these days only in the memory of the very old.

There was another smell, too – sweet and unmistakable and stomach-turning. The smell of frozen meat thawing out, as the ice-crystals that had preserved Edward Grace's body for so long gradually began to melt.

"This is amazing," said Jack, walking around. "I mean, why did this guy build a place like this? And right up here, where nobody could find it?"

Jim picked the notebook out of the hearth. The pages were gradually defrosting and coming apart. He used the blade of his penknife to open up the cover. In places the ink was badly smudged, but Edward Grace had written with a fine, clear hand, and almost all of it was decipherable.

Jack went around the table to the chair where Tibbles Two was sitting close to Edward Grace's body. He tried to stroke her but she ducked her head away. She remained where she was, staring at the gradually decaying ruin that had once been a man.

Jim took the notebook close to the fire and read the very first page:

February 8th 1921. I believe that I have discovered at last the means by which the malevolent spirit known as the Snowman may be finally appeased. It has taken me many years of [*illegible*] and psychic divination, but I now feel prepared to confront it and attempt to send it back to the Other World from which it appears to have sprung.

At this point, I feel able to make a full and true confession of my weakness and my [*illegible*]. I have been known since I booked my passage on the *Titanic* as Mr Edward Grace, of Bakewell, Derbyshire; but my true name is Captain Lawrence Edward Grace Oates – the very same Captain Oates who accompanied Captain Robert Falcon Scott on his ill-fated expedition to the South Pole.

I have read with unimaginable shame the stories of my heroism . . . of how I left the expedition's tent in a blizzard, in order to hamper the progress of my comrades no further. But none of the stories has mentioned that for days before this incident, we all felt that we were being accompanied by somebody who did not belong to our original party, somebody who always walked on our left, and who somehow helped to guide us through the worst of our difficulties. And of course nobody knew that when I was lying alone I was approached by this figure and offered my life, in return for the soul of the person who was dearest to me.

In my pain and my delirium, I accepted its offer. When I stepped out of the tent that night, with the blizzard in full spate, I did not walk to my death, nor did I have any intention of so doing. I walked instead into the arms of the Snowman, which creature carried me on its back to the nearest whaling depot. I sailed only a day later bound for

London, under the name of John Trethewen.

It was only when I reached London that I learned of the fate of my companions. I have to admit that there was a time when I contemplated suicide, particularly when I read about my own so-called heroism. But I had more urgent matters to consider. When I made discreet contact with my dearest love, Anthea Vane, she was overjoyed that I was still alive. But she told me that she had all manner of terrifying experiences, in which her apartments had been frozen solid, and a visitor had been trapped in her bath, the hot water of which had instantly turned to solid ice.

You have guessed, of course, that in my delirium at the South Pole, I had offered Anthea's soul to the Snow-man. I had never imagined that it would really seek to claim its fee.

I booked with Anthea a sailing to America on the *Titanic*, hoping to escape the Snowman by travelling to another continent. Who am I to guess that the Snowman was responsible for the tragedy in which so many people drowned? But I have learned since that the southward drifting of the iceberg which struck the *Titanic* was completely at variance with the winds and the tides and all predicted meteorological reports.

I lost my Anthea on the *Titanic*. She drowned in sight of me; and the Snowman claimed the soul which I had offered it.

That was why I came here to Alaska and built this house. I came here to study the Snowman and to learn how to destroy it for ever. I would live in this house, in the intense coldness in which the Snowman is always visible, and I would learn its ways, and its weaknesses, and in the end I would ensure that it never again preyed on those who are fighting for survival. I should have walked out of that tent in 1912, and allowed the blizzard to overwhelm me, as the legend tells it. I should have died at least with dignity. Instead, I sit here, bearing a guilt which is greater than any man can be expected to bear. For Captain Scott and all of my dear companions at the South Pole. For all of those hundreds of innocent souls who drowned on the *Titanic*. And I damn the Snowman, and I will engineer his downfall, even if I never live long enough to see it myself.

Jim lowered the notebook.

Jack looked at him in the dancing firelight and said, "Jesus."

But it was then that they both heard footsteps outside on the veranda. Footsteps, and the persistent tapping of a stick.

"It's here," said Jim. "It's come to collect its dues."

Fourteen

"Doesn't he tell you how to destroy it?" Jack asked, frantically. "What about all this stuff about sending it back to the Other World from which it sprung?"

Jim said, "Lock the door. Let's keep it at bay."

"Lock, no key," Jack reported.

"Bolts?"

"Bolts, yes. Bolts." He shot two large bolts, one at the top of the door and the other at the bottom. "That should hold it."

"Don't count on it. Let me take a look at this book."

Jim opened the notebook again. At the end of his meandering confession about what had really happened at the South Pole, and the sinking of the *Titanic*, Captain Oates had written in a very firm hand:

The Snowman is obliged to save those travellers in cold places who find themselves in danger. Therefore it can be destroyed by one who has courage enough to place himself in such peril that the Snowman is forced to attempt a rescue, and perishes as a result. If, for instance, you were to dive through a hole in the Arctic ice, the Snowman would be obliged to follow you, and if you made a particular effort to thwart its attempts to save you, the Snowman would drown, too.

206

The tapping on the veranda outside sounded louder; and the decorative stained-glass window at the side of the dining-room window suddenly frosted over. Tibbles Two sat up in her chair and her fur bristled.

"You understand what this means, don't you?" said Jack. "The only way to get rid of this thing is to kill yourself, and to hope that it's going to kill itself, too, in trying to rescue you."

"Well, I guess I could throw myself off the edge of the escarpment, on to the Ghost Salmon Glacier."

"But that's *cold*, right? This creature revels in cold. You might throw yourself onto the Ghost Salmon Glacier, and die; but this creature would probably love it. This creature *is* cold, incarnate. What did Laura tell you about fire?"

Jim clapped his hand on Jack's shoulder. "Actually, Jack, you're right. You're a genius. That thing out there is duty-bound to save me, no matter from what. If we burn this place down, it's going to have to come in and save me. It has to burn itself voluntarily, otherwise the magic doesn't work."

"But you're not going to stay in here while it all burns down."

"Of course not. You think I'm crazy? I just need enough of a drama to lure the bastard in here, and get it trapped."

Tibbles Two mewed, and stood up with her front paws on the dining-room table. Her late master was already beginning to smell like overripe blue-vein cheese and his tongue had dropped out from between his teeth, swollen and black, like a huge leech.

"You're right, too, TT," said Jim. "The sooner we do this, the better."

They heard the front door of Dead Man's Mansion opening with a low, lubricious groan, and a further persistent tapping as the blind spirit came searching for them. It tapped along the corridor until it reached the living-room, and for a few moments they heard it probing around the armchairs and the mahogany bureaux. Then it came back out again, and tapped its way over to the dining-room. It tried the doorhandle, and rattled it, but the door was firmly bolted.

It tapped, and tapped again, and rattled the handle harder.

Jim said, "Jack – out of the window. Quick. I'm going to set this place alight."

"I can't let you do this on your own."

"I want you out of here. It wants you much more than it wants me. It's supposed to save me, remember? From you, it wants your soul."

"I can't let you. You're only my teacher, for Christ's sake."

"*Only* your teacher? *Only* your teacher? Do you mean to say that I've sweated blood for all of these years in Special Class Two and I'm only your teacher? Your teacher is your *teacher*, Jack. Your teacher teaches you facts, opinions, maturity, morality, humor, tragedy, everything. Who should be here when your parents are both dead and there's some kind of terrible spirit trying to kill you too, if it's not your teacher?"

Jack stared at him in amazement. "That's what I *mean*," he retorted. "There's some kind of terrible spirit banging at the door and you get all fired up and start *lecturing* me."

At that instant, there was a loud crackling sound, and the door to the dining-room froze. Jim could see it sparkling with frost, and a crazed pattern of fractures appear all over it. There was a second's pause, and then the door was shattered apart with a single blow from the Snowman's staff. Over the steaming fragments came the Snowman itself, even taller than ever, its face completely concealed inside its hood, its eyes glittering. It stopped by the door and raised its staff high.

"I have come only to collect what is rightfully mine."

"No human being belongs to anybody, least of all a Sno-cone like you."

"His father made a promise. His soul belongs to me."

"His father wasn't *compos mentis* at the time. Besides, his father bought the farm out on the glacier. Don't tell me you didn't take his soul when you had the chance."

"His father's soul was not the bargain. I gave his father life, and in return his father freely offered me his soul."

Jim edged sideways, nearer the fire. "Look – I don't mean to disappoint you but this isn't going to happen. When a man dies, all his debts are wiped off the slate. That goes for souls, too."

The figure made a disgusting slavering noise inside its hood. "I was pledged his soul as a straightforward agreement. No money changed hands, no honor was impugned. I have a right to garner his soul and I shall have it."

"That's where you're wrong," grinned Jim. He leaned across and pulled one of the blazing chair-legs out of the fire. He walked calmly toward the drapes and set fire to them at the bottom, where they had once been lavishly braided, and now hung ragged and dry. They caught fire instantly, and Jim stepped backward to light the next set of drapes, and then the next.

"You will pay for this!" the figure roared at him, in a voice like a dozen tortured prisoners screaming at once. *"You will pay for this, and so will every single person you love!"*

Jim tossed another blazing chair-leg to Jack, and Jack set fire to the sofa and the small display cabinet, with its stuffed Arctic gulls in it, and big green eggs. Within a

209

few seconds, the whole dining-room was ablaze – chairs, side-tables, lamps, even oil-paintings. The atmosphere was so cold and so dry, up here in the mountains, that everything blazed as if it had been splashed in gasoline.

"No!" roared the figure, blindly lashing its staff from side to side. *"I shall have what you owe me! And I shall have you, too, whatever my master bids me to do!"*

Jim and Jack backed away from the figure as it came tapping its way toward them. Obviously it became blinder and blinder as the light and the heat increased – that was why it had been so blind in California. But as the heat in the dining-room rose from fifty degrees below freezing to four or five degrees above, the figure began to fade from sight. It was only visible to the naked eye in conditions of extreme cold. Now that the room was well above freezing, and growing hotter all the time, it vanished.

"Watch yourself!" Jim warned Jack. "The last thing I saw, it was making its way around the side of the table, toward you. Be careful – it wants you first!"

Over the spitting and crackling of the flames, it was almost impossible to hear the tapping of the Snowman's stick. Jim took hold of Jack's arm and led him slowly around the room, trying to make his way toward the door, so that they could both escape. The heat was becoming unbearable, and a row of glass vases on the mantelpiece suddenly exploded, in twos or threes. A large oil-painting of a Romanian woman suddenly lurched sideways, its frame already beginning to give off some pretty little flames.

They kept circling around toward the door, Jim waving his left hand in front of him in case they walked directly into contact with the invisible Snowman. They had almost reached the door and so far he hadn't even felt a bite of frost, or even a chilly draft. Jack said, "Two more steps, Mr Rook, and we're home free." The dining-room was beginning to fill up with dense black smoke, and all the glass panes in the display cabinets were cracking.

Tibbles Two dropped down from her chair and began to follow them. She may have been a mystical cat, but she obviously hadn't foreseen any death in her own cards, and she wasn't going to risk another of her nine lives fecklessly.

The dining-room had walls of fire. The huge mahogany server was alight, the books were alight, the table was alight. Poor old Captain Oates was alight, too, his figure bending forward over the table as the heat twisted up his already mummified body.

"Let's get out of here," said Jim. "I can't see any spirit surviving this."

As they reached the entrance hall, however, making for the front door, Jack abruptly shouted out, *"Annnhhh!"* and dropped to his knees. The next thing that Jim knew, he was sliding across the hallway on his side, as if something were dragging him. And, of course, something *was* dragging him, but in this kind of heat the Snowman couldn't be seen at all.

"Jack!" Jim shouted, but Jack was almost unconscious. He slid across to the stairs and began to bump up them, still on his side, his arms and legs dangling. It was like a weird act of levitation. Jim knew that the Snowman was dragging him, but he simply couldn't see him.

Unless, of course . . . He swung his rucksack off his shoulder, unbuckled it, and carefully pulled out Laura's mirror. He quickly buffed it with his elbow, then he spat to the north, and spat to the south, and spat to the east, and spat to the west. Then he spat in the mirror and said his own personal prayer. *"Mirror, mirror, I'll give you this spit . . . If you'll just show me this piece of—"*

He turned around, and held up the mirror – and there, just

for an instant, he saw the Snowman on the landing, pulling Jack toward one of the upstairs rooms. It must have been too hot downstairs for him to try freezing Jack to death.

Jim picked up one of the blazing table-legs and ran up the stairs after him. Jack was lying in the upstairs corridor, still half-conscious, his eyes flickering. But he wasn't moving any more. The Snowman must have let him go when it saw Jim running up the stairs, and now it was trying to hide itself. Jim lifted the mirror again, and quickly scanned the landing. There it was, standing in the far corner, those dried-prune eyes watching him sightlessly but conscious of his every move.

"You can't get away from me now!" Jim shouted at it. "I know what you are and I know what you have to do, whether you like it or not!"

"I will have this boy's soul first," the creature cautioned him. *"It has been owing to me for a very long time."*

But Jim walked into the bedroom directly in front of him. It had a tester bed with a frayed and frozen old canopy. It had thick drapes and net curtains. It had a large closet filled with old clothes. Jim whirled his fiery table-leg around and around his head until it really began to flare up. Then he touched the clothes and the bed-canopy and the nets and anything else that would burn. He stood in the middle of the blazing room with his back turned to the Snowman, but holding up Laura's mirror so that he could see it coming.

The fire in the bedroom spread even more quickly than the blaze in the dining-room downstairs. Before he knew it, the bed was a blazing funeral-pyre of wood and horsehair and curling springs, and the drapes were being eaten up by the fiercest fire that Jim had ever seen. The heat was growing intolerable, and the smoke was so thick that he was coughing and whining, rather than breathing in and out.

But he stayed where he was as the room burned even

more wildly all around him. In his mirror he could see the figure on the landing outside, torn between its greed to feed itself on Jack's immortal soul, and its duty to rescue Jim from any harm. Jim was an Arctic wanderer: no matter what threat he faced, the Snowman was bound by the terms of its punishment to save his life.

Still the creature hesitated. The fire was so hot now that Jim's stormproof coat was softening and melting, and his bootlaces were beginning to smoke. Sweat was running down his face and he could smell his hair starting to smolder. His cheeks felt as if they were actually burning, but he didn't flinch. If he gave in now, the creature would have them both.

The Snowman came nearer to the bedroom door. It stood with both its hands raised across its face, as if it were making a secret sign, or shielding itself from the heat. Jim could see it in his mirror but even that was becoming too hot to handle. The rug under his feet was glittering with tiny orange sparks and the wool was charring like old, burned flesh.

At that moment, Jack recovered. He dragged himself up on to one elbow and stared at Jim in horror. "Jim! Get out of there! Jim, your goddamned hair's on fire!"

Jim could feel the heat on his scalp and he patted it with his hand. The palm of his hand was filled with charred black hair.

Oh Christ, he thought. I've overplayed it this time. I'm going to roast to death, right here in this room.

Still the tall white creature held back. It turned again to look at Jack, and it lifted its hand as if to seize him and tear out his heart. But it hesitated, hesitated. It had made a promise to the Great Immortal Being and it couldn't deny it.

The soles of Jim's boots began to burn. But at that instant the tall white creature made a lunge into the blazing bedroom to rescue him. Jim saw the figure in Laura's mirror, its shoulders hunched, its arms outstretched, and for one split-second he thought that he saw its face. But as it tried to seize him, he sidestepped, and rolled over on the burning carpet, two quick rolls and he was out of the door.

The Snowman whirled around in the center of the room. *"You fool!"* it screamed at him. *"You will pay for ever for this!"*

But Jim slammed the bedroom door and twisted the key in the handle.

There was a furious beating on the other side of the door. Then the beating subsided, and they heard a low, agonized moaning. The moaning rose higher and higher, until it was a piercing, mock-operatic screech. It went on and on until Jim thought that it was never going to end and they were all going to go out of their heads.

Then something inside the room exploded. Maybe the creature was too cold to withstand such heat. Maybe there was ammunition in the room; or even a couple of sticks of dynamite. But the whole house shook to its foundations, and fragments of window-frame were sent tumbling into the snow-clouds far below.

Jim and Jack staggered down to the front door, and out into the freezing cold. Dead Man's Mansion was burning from basement to attic, with huge flames rolling out of every window. Its roof collapsed, sending showers of sparks up into the air, to join the stars. Then the upstairs floor fell in, followed by the stairs. They stood two or three hundred feet away, close enough to feel the heat of the fire, and watched as it brought down the greatest private house in northern Alaska.

Long after the main fire had burned itself out, and there was nothing left but smoking ruins, Jim circled the house whistling and calling. "TT? TT? Where are you, TT?"

But the cat didn't answer. Jim could only conclude that it had stayed with Captain Oates in the dining-room, and preferred the loyalty of death to the disloyalty of survival.

Jim put his arm around Jack and said, "Let's go. It's a long walk back and all of my Snickers have melted."

Jack said nothing, but turned and stared at the black, skeletal wreckage of Dead Man's Mansion. Then he tightened the straps of his rucksack and started to walk.

When he arrived at college the following Monday, Karen came across and said, "Jim! Look at you! What on earth happened? Your hair!"

"Little accident with a barbecue," he told her.

"How was your trip to Alaska?"

"Well, how do you want to put it? It was partly successful."

"Only partly?"

"I think I learned something. Not to interfere with other people's problems. Not to get involved in other people's lives."

"You're kidding me. I thought you loved interfering with other people's lives."

Jim walked across the parking-lot into the college building. As he turned into the main corridor, he saw Dr Friendly talking to Clarence, the janitor. He went over and waited until Dr Friendly had finished.

Clarence said, "Hey, Mr Rook! You look like you've been sunbathing – two inches from the sun!"

"Little accident with a barbecue," said Jim.

Dr Friendly said, "You're back, then. Successful trip?"

"In a way. I did what I set out to do. And I guess I discovered something, too."

"Oh, yes?"

"It's time I moved on. I can't stay with Special Class Two for the rest of my life. You don't support it, Dr Ehrlichman is only half-hearted, and what good am I doing, really? You're right: I'm giving my kids nothing but false hopes and expectations they can never hope to fulfil."

He paused, and then he said, "I called Madeleine Ouster over the weekend and I'm flying to DC at the end of the week."

Dr Friendly put his arm around his shoulder. "You know something, James. For the first time in your life, I think you're doing the right thing."

He sat in his classroom that afternoon and listened to his students analyzing 'The Ball Poem'. Then, when they were finished, he stood up and walked to the back of the classroom.

"What if the little boy had never had a ball to begin with? What if he had never had a ball to lose?"

"I don't get your meaning," said Tarquin Tree.

"Well, take *you* for instance. When you first came to this class, you'd never read a single book, you didn't know a single poem. You thought that Walt Whitman was a country-and-western singer. When you leave this class, I'll bet you money that you never pick up another book, and that you never read another poem. So what's the point of your coming here, and what's the point of my giving you that ball, when you and I both know that you're going to let it go bouncing off down the road, and lose it for ever into the harbor?"

"What's the *point*?" asked Tarquin, confused. "What's the *point*?"

"That's what I'm asking you, yes."

"There doesn't have to be a *point*, does there? Like, what's the point of anything? What's the point of music?

What's the point of red Corvettes? What's the point of sex, when you're not having babies? There doesn't have to be a *point*."

"I don't know," said Jim. "Sometimes, maybe there does. Sometimes you feel that your own life has to have a point. Sometimes you have to do something for yourself and put other people second. I have a gift, as you all know, a very great gift. I can see spirits and ghosts and things that people normally can't see. But it's like being a healer, in a way. Everybody comes and asks you to help them, and sometimes they don't even ask, but you help them anyhow, because you've got the gift and who are you to refuse anybody the benefits of it?

"But right now I want to go away and lead a life where nobody knows what I can see; and nobody knows what I can do. Right now I want to try to be an ordinary person."

"You're leaving us?" said Linda Starewsky, in disbelief.

Washington Freeman III shook his head and kept on shaking his head. "You can't leave us, man. What are we going to do if you leave us?"

"You're going to do exactly what you did before you met me. You're going to do the best you can."

"Yes, but who's going to teach us about all of those poems and stuff?" asked Billyjo Muntz. "You know – who's going to give us that, like, *insight?*"

"You have your own insight," said Jim. "Learn to rely on yourselves, instead of me. Look for your own poems. So long as you remember what I taught you – so long as you bother to read, and to think, and never to take anything at its face value – you'll get along fine."

Laura Killmeyer said, "Don't you believe in magic any more?"

"Sure I believe in magic. But magic doesn't solve

everything. Sometimes we have to sort things out the hard way, the ordinary way, without the benefit of magic."

He reached the back of the class. Nestor Fawkes was crouched over his desk, writing something in his awkward, spidery script. Jim stood over him for a while, and then said, "What are you doing there, Nestor? Mind if I see it?"

Nestor looked up. His shirt collar was grubby and there was a new red bruise on his cheek where his father had hit him. He handed the piece of paper to Jim, all folded up, and Jim took it back to his desk.

"All right, everybody. You just have time to start reading *The Rime of the Ancient Mariner* by Samuel Taylor Coleridge. Whatever your first impressions, this is a very strange spaced-out poem full of weird and powerful images."

Everybody made a noise opening their poetry books and scuffling their feet and whispering. Jim sat down and opened the piece of paper that Nestor had given him. It said, simply, *'Dont go. Please. Regards, Nestor.'*

Jim sat for a long time with his hand covering his mouth. When the recess bell rang he remained where he was. He watched his students file out of Special Class II, and Nestor was the last of all.

After a while Jim picked up his briefcase and left the room without looking back. Karen was waiting for him at the end of the corridor.

"What's wrong?" she asked him.

He shrugged. It was ridiculous, but he found his eyes prickling with tears. "Nothing," he said. "Somebody just stuck a knife in my heart, that's all."